# Atl Be The Day

\-

# The Road to

# Quantum Rubble

A Stephen Yobar Mystery

PATRICK B. MURPHY

Books by Patrick B. Murphy available on Amazon.com

Stephen Yobar Mysteries

SAE It Isn't So

Atl Be The Day – The Road to Quantum Rubble

Bryan Duffy Mysteries

High Voltage – A Bryan Duffy Mystery

Spring Time – A Bryan Duffy Mystery

Fall Break – A Bryan Duffy Mystery

Beyond The Pale – A Bryan Duffy Mystery

To Nancy,

Thank you for your kindness

# Chapter 0

# 14,500 years ago, northern Saskatchewan

The Leader carried a mammoth tusk slung over his shoulder. The surface of the tusk was inscribed with scenes of grassland, mountain passes, valleys, rivers; quarry of single prey, multiple prey; weapons of spears, rocks, stone knives; battle formations of two groups attacking, three groups attacking. The Leader would point to the pictures to describe his battle plan to the hunters. These symbols could be combined by the Leader into hundreds of different battle plans, though no one had ever considered calculating the exact number of combinations there were.

High skies and ragged newborn mountains painted the scene. The Hunter god traveled the sky, half-full, hungry. The air was cold and the grassland immense and the sky was clear and never-ending. The only way to survive was to hunt. Not even the most audacious dreamer in the

Group could imagine anything else. Mammoth bone tents were state of the art. What there was in front of you was all there was. All that stood between you and death was the Group.

He was in the Leader's hunting pack of nine men, creeping downwind along a line of tall grass. He squatted next to an outcropping of wildflowers, small purple leaves rising from the tundra. They blew softly on his shins. A small group of three mammoths drank at a nearby fast-flowing brook.

His left hand held his spear: a two foot-long wooden shaft with two rows of three descending stone blades starting at the tip. The blades were inserted in narrow grooves scraped with a fine stone tool, fastened with mammoth ligament. His right hand held the spear launcher: a mammoth bone with a sharp outcropping at the end of the bone that fit the back end of the spear. The spear launcher increased his distance, power, and accuracy greatly. Only the Leader could throw the spear better than he.

The hunters huddled closer to The Leader. The Leader pointed to a series of scenes and tactics on the mammoth tusk and then called the play: five fingers up on the left hand - five of them will go to the left. Four fingers upon the right hand: four will go to the right. As always, the Leader would launch his spear first then the others would follow. The Leader would take the prime cut of meat and the others would follow. The Leader would pick his mate and the others would follow.

He nodded his head with the other nodding heads in the hunting pack. For good luck, he rubbed the small stone disk held around his neck by a thin strand of bear gut. He crouched in the waist-high wildflowers, purple and yellow. As he stood up, the stone got stuck on a small twig; the strand broke and his good luck charm fell into the wildflowers without notice. The hunting pack flanked the mammoths on both sides. He broke formation and angled towards the Leader. The Leader launched his spear at the smallest mammoth. He loaded his spear into the hand launcher and hove it directly at the Leader's back.

Who's the Leader *now*?

# Chapter 1

"What a dump!" Stephen exclaimed, articulating each word like Liz Taylor, gesturing his right arm towards the dumping bins.

Danny shook his head. "Dad, you say that *every* time. It's like you're *trying* to drive me away."

Stephen smiled as he adjusted his work gloves and grabbed two garbage bags from the bed of his pickup. The truck had the magical county sticker that allowed him to use the Durham County dump – city dwellers need not come by. The truck had no air conditioning, no power brakes, and no power steering, but it had a sticker. And many dents.

As he approached middle age, the features of Stephen's face had begun to migrate. His eyes were fading away from his nose. His mouth smirked in a line unrelated to his eyes. His nose had started to grow again.

4

After the mystery "SAE It Isn't So" resolved earlier in the year, Danny had decided to be nicer to his father. "You can't take anything for granted" was his new motto.

Even still, it was hard serving up the softballs to his Dad. But off he went, well, because his dad's 48th birthday was about six months away – as good a reason as any to be nice. As Dad put it, he was going to be in his middle late forties.

"Dad, what do you think is the difference between ethics and morals?" Danny found an inner peace in knowing that he *asked* for this lecture which gave him the right to tune out as much as he could get away with. Now fully grown, Danny was at peace with his father after what he thought was a rocky upbringing. He stood a few inches shorter than his father, definitely a few inches shorter around the waist.

Stephen didn't mind Danny being nice to him, and he almost hesitated before he launched in. The slight stench from the garbage bins didn't inspire the brevity that Danny secretly hoped for.

Stephen gestured his right arm at the truck. "Ethically? You see that sticker on the windshield? It says I am allowed to dump my garbage here. If I didn't have the sticker, I could sneak in, or I could borrow someone else's sticker, but that wouldn't be ethical. I would be breaking the rules."

Stephen dropped his right arm and jabbed out his left arm, like the Scarecrow.

"But morally? I think morals are what happens between people. No person would get hurt if I used a sticker illegally, so it would be moral. Or almost *amoral*."

Leaning against the truck, Stephen said, "It's kind of like dark matter, son."[1]

---

[1] A moment after the Big Bang, the energy density of the universe (i.e., the energy in the primordial space-time quantum bubble that just ripped open) was too high to be sustained. Once the rip in space-time occurred, energy quantized and ran for its life. These high energy quanta were furiously looking for someplace that could accommodate their immense energy density. Meanwhile, in a desperate attempt to cool down to

manageable levels, the primordial space-time quantum bubble was spitting out new space-time quanta like soap bubbles being blown from a toy pipe. It would take a few more moments for enough space-time bubbles to be created to hold the intense energy. But what to do in the meantime?

In the shorter than Planck-length gaps between the space-time bubbles, there was a nearly infinite number of incredibly small, closed dimensional loops. They lived in the cracks between space-time bubbles and were 'invisible' to the space-time bubbles. The good news was that these closed loops could hold the high energy quanta that the space-time bubbles could not. High energy quanta jumped into the closed loops like kids jumping onto a rapidly spinning merry-go-round.

This was moving day in the fledgling universe! Within a few moments, most of the high energy quanta had been absorbed into the closed loop dimensions. The remaining energy quanta had cooled to a low enough energy level that they could be absorbed in space-time quantum bubbles without ripping them apart.

After a few more moments, the energy quanta that had jumped into the closed loops **expanded** to hit the walls of the closed loops. When all that energy hit the walls of the closed loops at the same time, the closed loops briefly **pushed** against all the space-time quanta around them. This *bump* by the close-loops against the space-time bubbles caused the 'inflationary period' in which the size of the space-time universe expanded at faster than the speed of light, from less than the size of a neutron to the size of a softball. If you think of a unit 'time slice' as $10^{-36}$ seconds after the Big Bang, then the inflationary period started at that point and lasted for at least 1,000 more of those 'time slices'.

After those miniscule moments, the average energy inside the space-time bubbles in the Universe had dropped to manageable levels. Most of the high energy quanta were now in the closed loops and the low energy quanta remaining in space-time settled into gamma rays, x-rays, quarks, electrons, neutrinos, and other elementary particles and energy manifestations in the universe we see today.

But whatever happened to the energy that was absorbed into the closed loop dimensions? We, inside space-time universe,

Before he could control himself, Danny uttered, "Huh?"

"Dark matter is invisible – another word for saying that we haven't found a way to detect it yet.  But we will.  Anyway, it accounts for almost half of the gravitational force in the universe.  But even though we can't *detect* it, we can see its *effects*."

Stephen paused and stroked his chin where his beard used to be.  "All this garbage here will be put in a dump.  It will degrade into smaller and smaller units until it won't degrade any more.  Not in our life time, anyway.  Ultimately it turns into rubble."

"Rubble?" Danny couldn't remember hearing anyone actually saying that word before.

---

perceive their effects today as gravity.  But since we can't see these small closed loops, we call them "dark matter".

"All the way down to quantum rubble,[2]" Stephen reinforced.

"It's what you *can't* see that's important, Danny." One more arm point at Danny. "That's how they get ya."

"But what if no one sees you?" Danny shot back quickly. Too quickly.

Now it was Stephen's turn to utter, "Huh?"

"Nothing, Dad, just pulling your chain. Let's go."

Stephen walked back to the truck and wondered, if all the light were removed from the universe, could a particle like a proton go faster than the speed of light? That is, if there were no light in the universe, must the speed of light

---

[2] Quantum Rubble
We hope to see the smallest unit,
The Quantum,
That tells us we've reached the Truth,
That we understand.
But our hopes fade away
Into quantum rubble.

be obeyed by other particles?  Or does law only apply when there *actually are* light photons in the universe?

When they had gotten in the truck, Danny could tell that Stephen was going to keep asking about him.  So a preventive strike was in order.

"So what's up with you and Merri?" Danny asked while looking straight through the windshield.

"It's Merrimac, not Merri."  The correction gave him a moment to think about Merrimac Edwards, the clinical research associate he had been dating for the last several months.  "She's great.  Her biggest flaw seems to be dating me."

"Is she why you cut your beard?"

Stephen stroked his chin and retorted, "What, this chin?  Pure and white as a flock new shorn, to quote a poem?"

"Where does all this garbage go, Dad?  I mean, how long does it take to... You know..."

"Disappear?" Stephen offered. "No, son, you can't hide things forever, even in the garbage."

Stephen cranked the engine. "Some last advice you're probably not expecting," Stephen concluded to Danny.

"Prepare for the best in case you get it."

# Chapter 2

Stephen Yobar wound his way through Ptolemy Institutional Review Board, Inc.'s myriad hallways to arrive at the central hub of the building. A huge conference room was the venue of their lucrative revenue source: running IRB meetings, including the one this afternoon. It was at IRB meetings like today's that human subject clinical trials obtained their legally required ethics board approval.

Stephen typically arrived twenty minutes early so he could enjoy his complimentary IRB member lunch. He walked slowly down the table holding the boxed lunches from *The Deli Box*, peered at their descriptions, weighed hedonism vs. asceticism, and eventually landed on a Thai chicken salad. With ranch dressing. And a cookie. He considered putting the cookie back for general consumption, but he decided that would be insulting to *The Deli Box*.

The large oak table filled up most of the conference room.  Each seat at the table had a laptop computer logged into the Ptolemy IRB website.  The board members used the website to review clinical trial documents and then voted to approve, not approve, or defer clinical trials. For today's board meeting, Stephen was the non-scientist; the regulations required that at least one non-scientist be on every board which votes on a clinical trial.

An ornately framed oil portrait adorned each of the four walls: Ptolemy, who in the AD 100s argued that heavenly objects revolve around Earth; Lady Mary Wortley Montagu, who championed small pox inoculations in 1718; James Lind, who ran the first clinical trial on vitamin C and scurvy in 1747; and Jonas Salk whose polio vaccine was introduced in 1955.

At his second or third IRB meeting, Stephen had pointed to the walls and asked the board chairman, "Hey PJ, this is a stellar bunch of portraits you have up here.  I can't help but notice that you don't have a data manager on one of these walls.  Now why is that?"

Grafe frowned, looked down, and pursed his lips, appearing to ponder the question carefully.

He raised his eyes back to Stephen. "Who would you recommend? Who is the most famous clinical trial data manager?"

After a few beats of Stephen's silent response, Grafe offered an awkward smile, nodded his head slowly, and started to walk away. Stephen stopped him.

"OK, OK, you got me there. But can you tell me why this company is called Ptolemy? It seems an odd name to me: an unscientific theory, Ptolemy saying that the sun revolved around the earth, being the namesake of a group that evaluates the science and ethics of clinical trials."

Grafe had his canned answer ready. "Yes, this company is named after Ptolemy who believed the sun revolved around the earth, a theory which is not in current scientific vogue. But for every IRB, ethics requires that everything *does* revolve around the research *subject*, not the research *study*. It is the role of the IRB to protect the rights of the research subjects. That protection is more important than the possible scientific benefit of the study."

Today, Stephen took his Thai chicken salad box to his corner of the table. There wasn't assigned seating, but members on Stephen's board tended to sit in the same places each meeting. Another reason to get there early – dibs on a corner.

As the committee chairman, PJ Grafe felt it was his responsibility to take advantage of the brief socializing opportunity during meal time so he started talking across the table to one of the long-time members, Dr. Borowsky, a neurologist from Duke.

"You were asking me, Jenny, about how I could have lost 20 pounds when I'm constantly in meetings with catered lunches." PJ (un)consciously patted his stomach which Stephen had to admit was smaller than it was six months ago. "I lost it by running every night on my neighborhood path, Mammoth Way. It runs right behind my house and it really is beautiful. It's a two mile loop that runs along Crooked Creek and that blueberry farm, a great perk for my subdivision. I think the running has even started making my white hair turn brown again." He scratched at the shock of white hair on his left temple.

That spurred a few moments of sidebar conversations for which Chairman Grafe gave himself credit as a successful team builder.

As Stephen reflected later, some successes can be taken too far. Dr. Borowsky took the opportunity to ask her colleague, Dr. Sutton Keyen, from Woodbridge, East Anglia, England, what he usually does over the Independence Day holiday weekend as it was approaching in a couple of months. Ribbing a Brit over the Revolutionary War was slightly farther than even Stephen would go.

Dr. Keyen pretended to take the comment in stride. He raised his eyes in a recollective position and said, "I'm not sure, but last July 4, I was digging for fossils in Duke Forest and I found a few flint arrowheads. Fascinating to see the history of the original inhabitants of this land."

While Stephen was deciding how to react to the *original inhabitants* jab, Dr. Keyen continued.

"That reminds me," Dr. Keyen started, "of one of the worst dates I ever had. It was near your Independence Day, but I was 18 and in England." Keyen paused his story and some others had started to listen. Keyen peered over his reading glasses at the clock on the wall and saw he had a few minutes before the meeting was to start.

Keyen turned his glance from the clock to Stephen. "As I said, we were both about 18 and we'd been dating for a month or so. By 10PM, we were parked in my car in a secluded spot with the radio on softly. There was a chill that night and soon enough the windows began to fog over inside."

The whole table was listening now.

"Just when she started to make her move, the most extraordinary thing happened. Slowly, before both our eyes, a footprint began to appear on the windshield. Two woman-sized footprints, to be accurate." Keyen paused.

"Things went downhill from there."

The small gathering of board members filled the room filled with laughs and shakes of heads. "That date was with the first future former Mrs. Keyen," he concluded.

Stephen took advantage of the last two pre-meeting minutes as he saw PJ Grafe franticly tapping his computer keyboard, no doubt rushing to start the meeting.

Stephen said to the group, "Well, if he can tell a story like that[3].... Can anyone help me to think of legitimate triple hyphenated words, like.... like saying a comedian's act is *Martin-Lewis-like*. Or an academic book is *Merriam-Webster-esque*."

No one had a response. He persisted.

"Or *woman-sized-footprint*, like Dr. Keyen just described, though I would argue that is really a quadruple hyphenated word because footprint has been combined into one word by slackers." To the silence, he continued,

---

[3] Stephen walked Merrimac to her door at the end of their date. The screen door closed as Stephen failed to make his move for their first goodnight kiss. After a few steps towards his car, he heard the screen door slam shut again. He turned back to the house and suddenly she was in front of him. She reached up to his cheeks with both hands and kissed him, smiled, and went back into her house.

"One could also argue woman is a compound word of *wo* and *man* with an invisible hyphen to make a string of five words, but..."

"Thankfully," PJ Grafe announced to the group, "I am calling this meeting of the Ptolemy institutional review board to order."

Grafe laid out the rules for the meeting.

"Confidentiality is in place from this point forward, please do not discuss the workings of the board outside of the board. If you have a conflict of interest on a proposed clinical trial, please let me know and you can leave the room during the discussion and vote. The previous meeting's notes have been approved. All non-board members, please leave and we will call you in when your study comes up on the agenda." Several people, including Dr. Keyen, left the room.

Grafe's role as chairman was to lead the group through the review of 12 clinical trials on the agenda. His technical specialty was pharmacology.

The first few reviews and votes went smoothly until Dr. Keyen's new clinical trial came up. Dr. Keyen was called into the room and sat at the corner across from Stephen. Stephen had been assigned as the primary reviewer for the clinical trial, Grafe was the secondary reviewer. Dr. Keyen was there to answer questions but would leave the room again before the board discussed and voted. Dr. Keyen's submission under review today was to become a site for a rare pediatric blood cancer clinical trial.

Before Stephen could begin presenting his summary of the clinical trial to the board, Grafe interrupted.

"Sorry to interrupt, Stephen, but I need to say something before you start."

Grafe was speaking to the group but he wouldn't look directly at Dr. Keyen.

"I reviewed this submission," he resumed, "and I think there is enough uncertainty in it that I can't let it come to a vote in the board yet. The informed consent seems to be missing a few required elements. Also, the FDA has released two updates on the side effects of the study drugs and those updates aren't reflected in the materials here. The safety results of two previous studies aren't included in the protocol or informed consent. We will have to have these, and about...." he looked down at his computer "...twelve other stipulations addressed before we can have a vote."

Dr. Keyen responded with a very strained voice. "I can get you the updates of the FDA releases, but I can't change the other materials myself, as you well know, because I am only one site out of thirty in this trial. It would take half a year to get changes through all the IRBs for the other sites."

"I understand that, Dr. Keyen," Grafe replied, hoping his voice was going to steer the discussion back to the center of the group. "However, this board is concerned with the protecting the rights of subjects for clinical trials we approve. That has to be our primary responsibility."

Grafe presented his conclusion as chairman. "We will review this submission again next month when all the stipulations can reasonably have been addressed."

Dr. Keyen turned irate. "I can't get all those stipulations approved by the other sites in a month! But I could get this study up and going in six weeks at my practice if the IRB approves. We can make it work! This is the third study of mine in a row that you're blocking! How can you justify slowing down research like this for no good reason?"

"I'm sorry, we have to move on." Grafe looked back down to his computer and moved on to the next clinical trial.

Keyen got up and stormed out of the room. The board approved a few annual continuing research requests and then Grafe called for a ten minute break.

Stephen wondered how Grafe was judging his team building skills now.

# Chapter 3

Parent/teacher nights at the Durham Friends School were Danny's favorite events.  Usually, there was excitement in the air and the stakes were high as parents see how their children are doing by visiting the classrooms and having short talks with each teacher.  Tonight's event was the end of year night.  As principal Dr. Nygren was fond of saying, the parents have to be happy to provide the tuition that goes to pay for teachers' sports cars. Danny was still limping along with his Spider convertible; the fact that it died on the side of the road while someone deliberately tried to run him over last year (in the mystery "SAE It Isn't So") wasn't the car's fault – the killer sabotaged the car in order to try to kill Danny.  Danny had tried to mentally distance himself from those events, which was easier than it sounds because that whole situation was so hard to believe.  But he was a bit off even now, though, because he had recently (sort of) broken up (kind of) with his (ex) girlfriend Brenda.

Two women in their mid-30s headed towards him in his crowded classroom. Mrs. Caruso smiled at Danny and said, "Hi, Danny. This is my good friend Ann O'Riley, her daughter Lara is one year behind Eric."

Danny and Ann shook hands and said hello.

Ann pointed to the brightly decorated walls. "You have a great classroom, Danny. I love all this art, but I thought you were a Spanish teacher?"

"Oh, but he uses so much art!" Mrs. Caruso proudly interjected. She looked around the room. "Wait, where is it…. there," she pointed, "by the bookshelf. Do you see? That's the moon picture Eric made last year which Danny so brilliantly noticed was genius!" The picture had different phases of the moon, each with a different expression.

Danny told the story to Ann. "I assigned an art project, combined with a written essay. Each student had to pick an animal and Eric wanted to do his on salamanders." Danny pointed to a salamander on his desk made from modeling clay and painted like the rainbow. "Someone had already picked that, as you can see. Eric said he wanted to pick the salamander because it would be easy and he didn't want to pick another animal. So I suggested the moon painting instead because Eric had asked about the English word faces and the Spanish word fases, like phases of the moon. Eric picked up on the idea and did a great job as you can see. Actually, the faces/phases bilingual pun reminded me a lot of my dad."

Ann looked back and forth between Danny and Mrs. Caruso and smiled. She could see why her friend was interested in Danny. Ann looked him in the eyes and continued, "I heard you were involved with investigating that stuff with Alexandria Knott last year. I've worked on a couple of projects with WDM, not with Alexandria, but with others. Thanks for what you did for her." Ann gave him a warm smile.

Some parents asked to squeeze by, the next class of parents was beginning to assemble.

Danny got a little embarrassed and looked at Mrs. Caruso to change the subject. "You know, I used to have a salamander when I was a kid."

"That's fascinating but not very interesting." Mrs. Caruso smiled at Danny, glancing over at Ann also.

Ann winked her ear at Danny. "I'm more interested in classical music than salamanders myself."

Danny thought for a moment and decided to try one of his dad's old jokes.

"My dad gave me a music box when I was little. The only thing it played was Minuet in D Minor."

Much to his surprise, a moment later, Ann actually did laugh. "I get it, a music box that only plays Bach's music." To Danny's knowledge, she was the only person who had ever gotten that joke.

"I heard you went on a long vacation to Asia last summer," Ann said to Danny while glancing at her friend. "I'm still planning for the summer. Where did you go? How did you like it? Are you going again?"

"Yes, I toured Asia and then came back through Europe. It's too long a story to tell before the next class meeting starts, but I had a great time there.[4] I recommend it."

Ann said goodbye and went off to her next class. Mrs. Caruso reached her hand out to shake Danny's and spoke softly. "Please come by the shop Friday around 7. We can have dinner."

---

[4] Best nightclubs: Beijing, Hong Kong

Favorite places: Taipei, Angor Wat

Best food: Taipei, Tokyo

Friendliest: Cambodia, Bangkok

Low key: Shanghai, Northern Vietnam

Best drinks: Vilnius

Best sushi: Tokyo

Most expensive: Hong Kong, London

Best architecture: Moscow, St. Petersburg, Tokyo

Safest: Moscow, Vilnius, Tokyo, Seoul, Hong Kong

Cleanest public transportation: Hong Kong

Places I couldn't get to: Singapore, the Philippines, Indonesia

Most famous person I saw: the Dalai Lama in Vilnius

# Chapter 4

Stephen hove a sigh of contentment as he awoke and realized it was Saturday morning.  Getting dressed, like everything else, was more relaxed on the weekend.  When he stood to pull his pants on, his belly pushed the elastic band of his underwear like a petulant child thrusting out his lower lip.

He heard the chickens squawking outside. I must have forgotten to shut them in last night, Stephen thought.  I guess I do think about chickens a lot, he admitted to himself.  While the water boiled in the coffeemaker[5], Stephen prepared for the upcoming Durham Wordplay contest: category is chickens – what expressions can be

---

[5] Coffee Pot Steam

Stultified love trapped, boils up finally
Blistering steam squeaks out sideways screeching
Heats the world, dances wildly, surrenders,
Softly subliming into quantum rubble.

used in the contest – go! Fly the coop. Don't count your chickens before they hatch. Hen pecked. Pecking order. Scratching out a living. Old biddy. Running around like a chicken with its head cut off. Don't chicken out. Fox in a hen house. Cooped up. Don't put all your eggs in one basket. Rule the roost. Birds of a feather flock together. Crowing. You're no spring chicken. Cocky. Strut like a rooster. That ain't chicken feed. Shake a tail feather. Not bad, he thought.

With the chickens pre-let out, Stephen called up Merrimac. It was almost eight so he figured she would be home from her morning run.

"Hey, good morning!" she answered the phone cheerfully.

"Good morning to you, Merrimac. How are you doing?"

"Pretty good. You usually don't call before eight. Is everything OK?"

"Yes, sorry. It's 7:50. That's 8 enough for me."

To her silence he continued. "I've got a pretty wild idea for us to do today. Are you in?"

Another short pause that Stephen often found hard to categorize as her hesitating or her waiting to see if he had more to say. "Hmm, depends on how wild."

Stephen started into his sales pitch. "OK, so last night, I went through all the gift cards I have in my wallet and my closet. Most of the cards have just a little money on them though some could still have a lot. I thought, I'll bet Merrimac would love to come with me on Saturday to redeem as many of these as we can. It'd be an adventure."

Merrimac thought, if that's his idea of adventure, then he definitely needs to get out more. Still in her early 30's, gift card-themed outings hadn't risen to the level of excitement that apparently they had for her new boyfriend. On the other hand, her plans for the morning including changing the oil in her car but she hadn't bought the materials yet. "Sounds like an adventure alright!" she rejoindered. "Hold on just a second." Stephen imagined her putting the phone down and her hair up.

"Ok, tell me tell what kind of cards we got here," she continued a few moments later.

"Great! I'll pick you up at nine!" He figured it was best to press on without details.

He picked her up and they decided to start in Raleigh and then work their way back to Durham. I-40 east on its way to Raleigh had no traffic through Research Triangle Park on Saturday mornings. When he hit Raleigh, he chose to drive down Hillsborough Street and see NC State's main campus. It was quiet and pretty – students all in the library, no doubt. On the Morgan Street roundabout, he exited down a small side road and parked about two blocks from the *Irregardless Café*.

They sat across the room from the sax player who had a JBL speaker system playing his backup music. As they drank their coffee and waited for French toast and huevos rancheros, Merrimac asked Stephen a question.

"So, do you like this place because of the food or because of the name? I know you well enough now that you're not going to let a name like *Irregardless* slip by without a comment."

Stephen smiled. "Yes, you do know me, Merrimac! I admit the name has bothered me since I first came here." He wanted to say *first came here decades ago,* but he was worried it would make him sound too old.

"But I'm very flexible, you see," he assured her. "Just like with the *Savvy Café*. Conveniently located in *Triangle Square*." The food was good and they lingered for half an hour listening to the saxophonist.

From there, it was a short drive to the North Carolina Museum of Art where he had two free special exhibit admissions left on his gift card. After an hour in the museum, they took a walk through the grounds. They kissed in a secluded area behind the stage where they projected movies onto the wall of the museum on Friday nights in summer. On their way out of Raleigh on Hillsborough St., they stopped at "Reader's Corner" where

Stephen finally cashed in his store credit which had been on a receipt in his wallet for over 15 years. A copy of Wallace Stevens's collected poems and *The Road to Reality* by Roger Penrose finally closed his account. Merrimac picked up a book on Southern cooking and a book on beekeeping.

It took about 35 minutes on I-40 west and the Durham Freeway north to get to downtown Durham. The first stop on the list downtown was to get a free cup of ice cream at *Parlour*. *Parlour* was next to the Bull Statue plaza. The bronze bull, the symbol of Durham, was about eight feet tall and ten feet long and was typically covered with children. The plaza was currently filled by yellow and green electric bikes for rent. They sat by the bull and ate their ice cream while Stephen told Merrimac what it was like playing in the parks with Danny when he was young. Their favorite was a dinosaur park and Danny used to climb all over the sculptures. The dinosaurs weren't as anatomically correct as this bull was, Stephen thought but wisely did not say.

Merrimac tried imagining Stephen so young. "Did you have the beard then?" she asked.

"No, that started about five years ago when I was on a trip and didn't have a razor so I decided to go for it."

"You look nice without it," she smiled at him.

They sat for a few moments and then Stephen stood up and rubbed his knee. "On to *Motorco*! Which color bike do you want – lemon or lime?"

Stephen used his app to rent two lemon bikes and they rode a mile or so down Rigsbee St. towards *Motorco*. Two blocks from *Motorco*, they stopped at the *Flip and Sip*, an axe throwing establishment with a full bar. Danny had gotten Stephen a gift card for his last birthday.

They parked their bikes and Stephen ended their trip on the app. Inside, they signed the injury waiver and went to the area where people were throwing axes. The stalls looked like basketball shooting arcades. Some newcomers were throwing the axes too softly and they bounced awkwardly off the target at dangerous angles. One guy was throwing it hard and it was making solid contact around the bullseye almost every time.

The bulls-eyes were about 15 feet from where you had to throw the axe.  Merrimac thought the one-handed technique looked the best and asked the manager what she thought was the best technique.  The manager talked them through the row of pictures that lined the hall from the throwing area to the bar.  She described each technique: two-handed over the head, one-handed overhand, underhanded.  There was even a picture of a customer dressed in costume that they let shoot arrows at a target outside.  Stephen asked the manager how common axidents are.  She missed the joke, but Merrimac noticed and wondered if that was a good thing or a bad thing.

After a few unsuccessful axe throws, they walked a few blocks to *Motorco* where Stephen used the gift card he got for competing in the Durham Wordplay contest last year. They bought some wings at the food truck across the street and sat on a park bench inside what used to be a garage bay.  The waiter brought them each a pint of

Paycheck lager from Fullsteam, brewed across the street as well. The garage door was rolled up so they could feel the breeze.

"Have you seen Danny recently?" Merrimac asked.

"We went to that French restaurant Rue Cler downtown last week and had lunch," Stephen said.

"I've never been there but I've heard a lot about it. It's right across from the puzzle room place. How was the food?"

"Great until the end when we ordered coffee." Stephen had that lilt in his voice that Merrimac had come to recognize.

"What happened?"

"We ordered iced coffee but it *chaud* up hot." He followed up with a look.

"I don't think you should assume people know French, Stephen." Merrimac suppressed a sneeze as the waiter came by to offer them dessert.

"The special today is chocolate cake. It's made from scratch," the waiter suggestive sold.

Stephen put that look on his face. "Sorry, I'm allergic to scratch."

"You are not! No one's allergic to scratch." Merrimac objected with a laugh.

"I am, too: it makes me itch."

Merrimac shook her head. The waiter walked away to settle the bill, no doubt thinking *The customer is always right*.

"OK, Stephen, just for that you have to answer a serious question. What's the most important thing that's happened in your life?" She leaned on the bench with her head in her hand.

Stephen tried to answer without a joke, but in the end he compromised with the truth and a joke.

"I'd have to say that fathering a child was the seminal event in my life."

# Chapter 5

Danny was parked in his Spider waiting for Mrs. Caruso's store, "Bedini's Dresses", to close at 7PM. The store was in the bottom floor of Erwin Square, a large squat building a few blocks off Ninth Street. He listened to a cassette tape he had made from one of his father's old records. Even though a few of the songs had skips in them from the inevitable vinyl scratches, they sounded much better than the iTunes versions. After all these years he found that he could still predict each skip. When Mrs. Caruso heard the tape on their first date, she asked him, "Why don't you get a digital copy of these songs instead of an old tape?" Danny replied, "This tape was made from one of my father's albums.[6]"

The tape ended and it still wasn't even quarter to 7 so Danny went into the coffee shop next door to Mrs.

---

[6] When I was little, Dad would sit on the carpet in the living room and play his albums loud. I would dance around and he would sing. I danced on the green cushioned seat that topped the bookcase under the window. Dad was laughing.

Caruso's store.  It was really more of a bakery than a coffee shop, especially given the name "The Boss's Basset Underground Bakery", owned by one of his friends Caroline Dunord.  They went to high school together, and their mothers both grew up in Yadkin county in western North Carolina.  Last month, he helped Caroline with the chalkboard outside her shop, stealing one of his dad's old jokes: "Come on in!  We knead the dough!"  Caroline had recently added ice cream making to the operation, calling it *The Daily Churn*.  Danny reminded himself to ask his dad for a pun for that.  Throw the old man a few softballs every now and then, it might help my karma.

Danny ordered his coffee and Caroline came out from the back to talk for a minute.

"How you doing, Danny?  Here for the coffee or the proprietor next door?"  She smiled at him and for some reason he squirmed a bit.

"Both, probably," he turned and scanned the room.

The wood floors were catching the last late afternoon sun.  The lights hung from exposed wooden joists high in the ceiling. Edison would approved of the long glass tubes though he would have preferred them powered by direct current rather than alternating current. Customers sat at rough wooden tables. The forest green walls were lined with painted cross-hatches that would make the Tudors feel at home. A few lucky tables had a hanging green lamp that gave extra light to the readers. The bottom halves of the windows were draped with burlap hung by copper rings on brass rods. A small pewter cup, with a lip curling downward like a spout that pouts, held the coffee cream on each table. Mirrors on the back wall reflected the curbside trees giving the illusion of a back deck.

The decorating leaned heavily towards pictures of basset hounds and blood hounds - some with more skin on their face than seemed possible. Other portraits were reminiscent of the Hush Puppy dog that adorned the shoes of his father's generation. A blackboard in the corner had writings from the regulars – thoughts, poems, jokes punctuated with a few photos[7].

A few tables towards the back were populated by regulars – people reading their newspapers, nibbling on a piece of pie, satisfaction and contentment mixed with blackberry filling on their faces. The regulars weren't an iPhone crowd. The bakery was a sanctuary from the world that had passed them by.

He turned back to Caroline and changed the subject. "Hey, did you sign up for the Durham Wordplay Contest? Dad thinks he's going to win it every year, but alas, he is winless."

Now it was her turn to look unsure. "I'm not sure," she said. "It sounds pretty nerve racking up on that stage."

---

[7]

The heron stalked slowly on Solstice Day,
Too cold and hungry to be scared away.
At the back of the pond, thorned tree limbs fell
And hid our visage like a magic spell.

The heron stalked slowly on Solstice Day,
The farm dog ran up and scared it away.
Loping up slowly to a pine tree peak,
A lone fish flapping in her bright blue beak.

"No, you definitely had the sense of humor for this contest. You'll do great. It's coming up quick so you better register to compete." They said goodbye and she returned to the back of the store.

Danny had tried to bring his dad here but his dad loved the Savvy Café and would only frequent that one coffee shop. It hit him that his dad was a pretty loyal guy on all fronts. He drank the coffee and saw it was 7:05, the dress store should be closed now.

He walked next door to "Bedini's Dresses" and gave the door a pull but it was locked. Danny knocked and waited with a smile as Mrs. Caruso walked to the door and let him in. She greeted Danny with a kiss and quickly locked the door again. Danny couldn't tell if she was trying to keep something out or trying to keep something in.

The first thing Danny saw on the wall was a huge black and white portrait of a man in his mid-30s, impeccably dressed in a top hat, white tie, and tails. Bedini's smile filled the room more than 80 years after the portrait had been made. Beneath the photo, the following lines were written:

"Our Founder, Alberto Bedini, Had the Following Motto:

For the man, the top hat.
For the woman, the dress."

"That's a funny sign, that man Bedini," Danny said as he slowly walked through the store looking at all the decorations.

"I just put a new one inside the dressing room that is even better," Mrs. Caruso said with a smile as she took his hand, turned her back on him, and slowly walked him into the dressing room.

The dressing room door locked with a loud click.

What about Brenda?  We broke up, but that was just three months ago - what if she wanted to get back together?  Mrs. Caruso had her hands on his shoulders and her body close to his.

Is the door really locked?  Mrs. Caruso was pulling him down to kiss him, pressing herself against him.

At a critical moment, Bedini's face peered at him from the wall, announcing another one of his seemingly endless supply of mottos:

"I will not accept any excuses.  Not even the truth!"

# Chapter 6

Stephen parked at his usual spot in Triangle Square. He was a few minutes early for his Tuesday coffee date with Merrimac. He decided to take the opportunity to go into Threads, an eyebrow threading shop which just opened up next door to the Savvy Café. A young woman with various facial piercings approached him and asked, "Are you looking for anything in particular?" She used her skeptical smile.

"No," Stephen couldn't resist, "Just browsing."[8]

When he stepped back outside, Merrimac had just parked and was walking towards him. After a brief but sincere hello kiss, they entered the coffee shop and sat at their usual table by the window. Stephen walked over to the proprietor Eduardo Tuttlehoff at the bar. The Tut was

---

[8] Merrimac's brown eyebrows.

wearing tight black biking shorts, but he didn't seem as concerned about it as Stephen was.

"What's new these days, Tut?" Stephen asked. He almost asked, "How's it hanging?" but he already knew the answer to that.

"I just got this fancy tea imported from Japan," Tut pointed to the jar on the bar. "They charge by the amount of time it stays in your cup. It's so strong that one bag can make several cups."

"How much is it?"

"It's three dollars for every minute you use. I recommend five minutes to get the full effect. Fifteen dollars total."

Stephen shook his head and said with a smile, "That's a bit too *steep* for me." To the Tut's unamused face, Stephen said, "How about the usual for Merrimac and me? Thanks." The Tut started on the double espressos.

Stephen leaned on the bar and stole a glance over his shoulder. Today, Merrimac's long hair was in its occasional bun.  Her blue shirt buttoned to the neck.  Her red cheeks from her dawn runs.  Her serious look when they talked about work, nestling the outer edge of her right index finger in her philtrum while thinking deeply.  Her crinkly eyes when her laughs burst out.  Her *I know, I know sotto voce* in agreement when they talked, punctuated with a slight head nod in the right direction.  Her pacifism, her potential for greatness, her engagement in new ideas, her kind eyes.

The Tut cleared his throat loudly and Stephen turned back to the bar and saw the two small saucers each with a demitasse cup of espresso.  He picked them up with a little noiseless noise.  He often thought of John Keats when she was nearby.

Before returning to the table, Stephen asked Tut, "Hey, what was your investment strategy that let you retire and start this restaurant?  I've got a few years left to go, though, but you got out by 60."

Tut smiled and held up a finger.  "One: buy the dream, sell the reality.  I like to buy trendy stocks and sell them before they're tested fully in the market. I've lost out on some big gains, but I've also escaped some big losses."

Two fingers. "Two: pigs get fat, hogs get slaughtered. This kind of goes with the first one really. It really means, don't get too greedy. You should keep that in mind, my friend." He ended with a short stab at Stephen's chest.

Stephen brought the coffees back to their window-side table. Most of their coffee went slowly as they caught each other up on recent news. After a few minutes of quiet broken only by the *caws* of the parking lot birds eeking through the window, Merrimac started humming a happy song to herself.

Stephen looked at the birds quietly, wondering if the humming relaxed him more than her. After a moment, she turned her glance to Stephen, touched his hand with a smile,[9] and then went back to her coffee. The Tut walked by and asked if she wanted another cup of coffee. She shook her head and added No, thank you. A moment later, she resumed humming. Stephen vowed that it wouldn't be him that broke the moment no matter how long he had to look out the window. Eventually she took in a deep breath, no doubt how they say to do it in yoga class, and started talking again.

After they were finished with the coffee, Stephen took the plates, cups, and demitasse spoons over to the bar. The Tut said, "Where's Danny these days? I haven't seen him in a couple of weeks. You two used to be like clockwork here on Thursdays." Stephen reached up to fake scratch his head so that he could steal another glance

---

[9]

Love flows softly from your warm fingertips
You smile wide with your eyebrows and cheeks,
I hope you can't hear my heart beat so loud
How did the world just collapse into us?
When you look me in the eyes I won't breathe
I don't want to distract your attention.
As you look away the moment passes
And our special slice of space-time is gone,
Surviving only in my mind and soul.
Safe, softly shielded from quantum rubble.

towards the booth. Looking out the window, Merrimac unconsciously loosened her hair scrunchie and her hair fell down. Seeing the birds fly away, she raised her hair off her shoulders and let it slowly unfurl falling through her fingers. The Tut proclaimed, "You're a fool."

Stephen broke his reverie and he turned back to the Tut. "What?"

"Do you have *anything* in common with her?" Tut stared at Stephen.

Stephen thought,

*Ode to Neutrinos*

*Two neutrinos, near each other*

*Happy with their independence, transferring their cargoes of quantum energy,*

*Conserving symmetries in equations and reality.*

*They laugh at the gravitational force!*

*Their masses so small that they hardly interact,*

*They tease gravitons with a 'come hither' look but then fade from view*

*Near Planck's Hideaway.*

*They scoff at the electromagnetic force!*

*It is not in charge of them!*

*Photons don't even bounce off,*

*Just phase on by.*

*They wipe their brows in relief that the strong force*

*Takes a mighty swing and misses - twice!*

*First, body shots at the quark distance*

*Followed by a roundhouse punch at the proton distance.*

*Swish, swoosh.*

*The weak force? Aye, there's the rub.*

*Neutrinos hurtle when a quark transforms,*

*From up to down, from top to bottom, from strange to charm.*

*And when you change a quark, you change a world.*

"Yes," Stephen answered. "We have some little things in common."

"Really?" Tut shot back. With a smirk, he put the dishes into the plastic tub. He laughed and walked back to the microwave which had just beeped.

# Chapter 7

My office that year was in the Caheunga Building on Market Street overlooking the Bull Statue plaza in downtown Durham. The high window opened up onto a small balcony with potted manzanita and eucalyptus trees. They belonged to the super but I took care of them. When they came inside last winter, we got on good speaking terms.

I was looking onto the plaza, noticing the new rental lemon and lime bikes in neat rows, scanning the crowd for dangerous women, when my buzzer rang. I had insisted on the buzzer when I signed the lease.

The breeze was blowing the eucalyptus scent into the office. I pressed the desk buzzer to open the front door and my potential client walked in. She was a young woman in her mid-twenties. She looked like she could be the daughter of my next door neighbor, if I had a next door neighbor, but I lived in the room adjoining my office. She was serious looking with glasses and had her black hair pulled back into a pony tail. She didn't have a purse. Her clothes fit loose and comfortably and nondescript, Old Navy *chic*. I stayed standing and invited her to sit in the chair across from my desk. The desk was too big for the office but it was my father's and I didn't know what else to do with it. She didn't seem to notice.

After her silence and declining my offer of coffee, she said, looking down, "My brother served two tours in Afghanistan and now that he's back he's hooked on opiate pills. He started taking them for an injury and post-traumatic stress disorder, but's he's not getting them from a doctor anymore and he can't quit. He gets them in prescription bottles with no names on them."

I nodded to her though she didn't see. This wasn't the first time I'd heard a story like this.

"What would you like me to do?"

She lifted her head. "I want you to find his dealer and kill him." She said it with a thin anger in her voice and intense eyes. Her glasses slipped but she didn't react.

"I understand how you feel," I said, "but I can't do that. But I will see what I can do to dissuade the dealer and introduce him to the police."

She pursed her lips and nodded OK. Her glasses slipped again and this time she did reposition them.

"Where does your brother live? Do you have a picture of him?"

She took the phone out of her back pocket. It was in a case with her ID, credit card, and some cash. She showed me a picture of her brother, it was the screen saver on her phone. He looked like a good kid, too young to be a two-tour vet with an opiate monkey on his back. I took a picture of her screen.

"He lives with my parents, in the basement. They know he has a problem but they don't know what to do."

I handed the phone back to her. "Where do you think he gets the pills?"

She had the answer to that quickly. "He gets them at night on the 2$^{nd}$ Friday of the month. He leaves home at

8PM. I know that's when he gets them because my parents say that the next day, Saturday, he binges on the pills and won't come out of his basement room." Her glasses seemed to jump upwards this time.

I noticed it was a little after 4PM on the 2$^{nd}$ Friday of the month. She was right on time.

"Where is your brother now?"

"He's at my parent's house. He works in the yard and garden most days."

She gave me the address. She hadn't asked my rates yet but took out a credit card and handed it to me. I put my palm up and asked her to text me her phone number and email address. I gave her my card.

"We can settle this when I see how long it's going to take," I said as she put my card in her phone case. I was probably going to give her the discount rate: a pepperoni pizza and a beer at Blaze Pizza. I'd just gotten a large check from the North Carolina Mutual Insurance company for proving fraud on a break-in so I could afford the roasted squash salad myself.

"I'll follow him tonight.  Does he have a car?"

"No, he uses Uber or Lyft.  At least he doesn't drive when he's under the influence," she said with pride. "He's a good man, he was a great soldier."  She looked me straight in the eye.  I liked that.

I asked her if she wanted a cupcake to go, I had a box from Orange cupcakes across the street.  She said no again, the folly of youth.  Or maybe she was holding out for bacon covered maple donuts from Duck Donuts.  It was hard to discern the millennials.

After she left, I googled her parent's house, it was in Woodcroft, a development which didn't live up to the adage that the name of the development should reference what it destroyed.  There actually were woods and large trees left by the developers.

After an early dinner of salmon, mashed potatoes, and sautéed spinach at Rue Cler, I made the ten minute drive down the Durham Freeway to I-40 west, exited at Fayetteville St., and turned left into Woodcroft.  I parked a block or so away from the address she had given me.  The house was on a corner and the street dropped steeply which allowed for a pretty good sized basement. Around 8PM, an Uber showed up and the brother walked from the house into the car.

He looked to be in his late twenties, five ten, 180 pounds. He had short hair, but not military short. He had several tattoos on his forearms, nothing unusual for these days. I gave them a minute head start and followed them back to downtown. The Uber dropped him off in front of a music club/bar across from the Durham Performing Arts Center called the *Flat Fifth*. I parked and went in.

I asked for a seat at the bar, which made the hostess happy because there were no tables available. The bartender was a young woman with pink hair and more than the minimum number of piercings. I ordered a brown ale on tap from Fullsteam Brewery which was just a couple of miles north of the bar. She asked if I wanted something to eat.

"How's the food here?"

She responded, "You should try the fried catfish and collards.  Best in the Triangle."

"Hmm," I said, "the menu has changed from the last time I was here a few years ago.  Back then, this place wasn't called the *Flat Fifth*, it was the *Sharp Fourth*."

She did a pretty good job of acting like she didn't get my joke.  "Well, the food's pretty good now," was all she could offer back.  Better than, "OK, Boomer", I guess.  I ordered the fried catfish strips and a side of the collard greens.  They didn't disappoint.

Between the bar and the bandstand was a sea of small tables, all of them filled.  A quintet was on the stand playing a bluesy version of *Violets for your Furs* though I preferred Coltrane's version.  A hat-wearing trumpet player was standing waiting for his turn, tapping his foot and smiling.  The balding bearded sax player was leaning into his tenor, finding his way to resolution.  The young guy playing the drums was laying it down, looking down and away with eyes closed.  The bass player and keyboardist flanked the older sax player, they looked like a duo.  The sax player stopped, and nodded to the slight applause.  Then the hat-wearing trumpeter took off.  After a few minutes, I decided that he was worthy of his hat.

The brother was standing at the other end of the bar and had also ordered a beer.  I watched him walk his beer to a table that was occupied.  The guy at the table was in his late forties, white, and had some grey in his otherwise dark hair.  It looked like the brother was asking the older dude if it was OK for him to sit down at the table.  He nodded OK and motioned for the brother to sit down.  The older guy was done eating anyway; there was a to-go box and a check holder on the table.

In the middle of the next number, I watched the brother pick up the check holder, open it, and put in what looked like three C notes, and then lay the check holder down again.  A moment later, the brother picked up the to-go box and left the club, leaving the three hundred behind.

I stayed and looked at the guy the table.  That switch was pretty slick and it looked beyond him judging by his face.  I started taking pictures with my phone.  A few minutes later, he took the money out of the check holder and put it into his pocket.  At 9:30, he ordered a piece of cake and paid with a credit card.  A new black check holder was put down on his table next to his cake box.  A few moments later, he took a small medicine bottle from his pocket and put it in the cake box.  At exactly 10, another guy in his late twenties came to the table, sat down, put money in the black check holder, and left after a few minutes with the bottle in the to-go box.

It played out again at 10:30.  By this time I had seen enough and taken enough pictures to get started.

I was going to come back next Friday night for more surveillance – no doubt, another crowd of vets picking up the check for this scumbag.  I'd bribe a waiter to bring me a glass or some silverware that he used so I could get some prints and run him down.

On Monday, I reported back to the sister that I had a handle on what was going on and that I'd have some good news for her hopefully next week.  I did a search on opiate deaths in the Triangle area over the past six months and found three former military members who had died of overdoses.  If this guy was involved, I'd make him feel like a ruptured spleen before I turned him over to the boys downtown.

# Chapter 8

The late spring air was cool as he lay in wait in the tall grass and flowers on the subdivision side of the Mammoth Way walking path that was the border between the blueberry farm and the subdivision. His buckskin shirt and kilt blended in perfectly with the brown tall grass. There was about an hour of sunlight left.

The past three evenings, he had hidden in the tall patch of wildflowers and deadnettle and watched his quarry Grafe run by. He observed from the same spot each night, satisfied that he couldn't see his previous evening's moccasin footprints. As he waited this evening, he rubbed the small stone circle hanging by a thin string from his neck. That bastard looked like he was enjoying his runs even as he was killing people each day. Not pulling the trigger, but just as guilty. Tonight was the night that would end.

As he saw Grafe turn the corner on Mammoth Way path, he loaded his handmade spear into the atlatl, attached the banner stone, and called out, "Hey, you!" Grafe stopped and turned to the sound coming from the grass, looking for but not seeing the source. He stood and planted his moccasined feet, steadied the spear in the back notch of the atlatl, used the banner stone to balance the atlatl, and hurled the spear at Grafe's chest with deadly accuracy. Grafe fell and was dead before his killer finished the short jog to recover his spear. Just to make sure, he slammed the banner stone into the side of Grafe's head. Quickly, he dragged Grafe into the woods halfway between the path and the farm, not noticing that the stone circle had been pulled from his neck by a branch.

Let's see him try to ruin someone's life *now*.

# Chapter 9

Danny lifted his right hand to knock on his father's door.  He had come to talk to his father about his relationship with Mrs. Caruso.  It was getting intense and he had to talk to someone, even if the price was listening to what his dad would have to say (and say and say) about it.  Stephen suggested discussing it over a homemade dinner.  An emotion jabbed him in the eye, forcing out a quick tear.  But he tucked it away again by the time his right hand came down on his father's door as a loud rap.

Stephen opened the door and greeted him with, *"Beside the lake, beneath the trees, fluttering and dancing in the breeze*.  Wordsworth.  That's where Merrimac and I are headed this weekend, out to Jordan Lake."  As always, Stephen waggled his fingers as he said *fluttering and dancing.*

Well, enough about me, Danny thought to himself as he headed to the fridge for a beer. Bad Penny lager, one of Danny's favorites.

"What's for dinner, Dad? Not sausages and grilled peppers and onions again I hope. They're not good for your colon! That diverticulitis had you down for a week last time."

Stephen had it ready, "My colon can kiss my ass!"

"What then? Hamburgers? Or pizza?"

Stephen rose only partly to the bait. "It's stacked tortillas tonight." He went into the kitchen to start cooking with only the slightest of limps in his left knee. With that certain sound in his voice, he said, "I would never serve you a lame male meal like hamburgers."

"Dad," Danny said to his retreating father, "why do you say things like that? Nobody gets them."

"People from ancient Mesopotamia, like from Elam, would get it. But I don't want to babble on."

Stephen reached down into a cabinet for a large iron skillet. "Anyway, people should always be listening for anagrams. At least I didn't say that I was partnering potatoes with hamburger because potatoes are a tame meat team mate."

"For once, Dad, we agree." He sat on the couch and looked at his phone while Stephen started cooking.

Stephen placed the iron skillet on the stove, filled it with corn oil, and heated it until a water drop popped on it. He fried a dozen small corn tortillas till they were hot, soft, and saturated with corn oil. He laid each tortilla on a plate, separated from the previous tortilla by a paper towel. Next, he cut an onion, a red pepper, and grated half a stick of sharp cheddar cheese. He drained the corn oil from the skillet and then browned a package of Morningstar black bean burgers, spicing it with Cajun seasoning, chili powder, and garlic. He mixed enchilada sauce and tomato sauce in a large glass bowl. The ingredients prepared, began the manufacturing process.

He set out four circular cake baking pans and began stacking the ingredients: a cooked tortilla dipped in enchilada sauce, diced onions and peppers, cooked black bean burger pieces, cheese, and then the same layer again, and then topped with a third tortilla. The crown was embellished with medium salsa, cheese, the remaining onions, and any remaining space was covered with taco sauce. Stephen put them in the oven for 35 minutes of baking.

"OK", Stephen said with a sigh as the oven door slammed shut. "Tell me what's up while I finish."

Danny started with the family, "How was your day?" first, to get things started.

Stephen pointed a spatula at him as he replied[10]. "You know that feeling where you think your glasses are about to break? They bend too much, start feeling loose? The threat hangs in the background of the day, lurking, perhaps negligibly, but definitely a negative vibe."

---

10

My eighteen dimensional quantum field equation
With my unique combination of parameter values
Perfectly describes me down to the random chances
Fluxing through my life.
My wave function accretes a diaphanous husk of quantum rubble.

Danny long ago stopped feeling obliged to respond to statements like that from his father.  Stephen flourished the spatula at him again, then again, then finally relented without another word.

So much for small talk, Danny decided, and started talking about Mrs. Caruso while Stephen diced fresh tomatoes, cilantro, and limes for a salsa and sliced iceberg lettuce and avocadoes for garnishing.  Danny said that she met her ex-husband at a Renaissance Festival 15 years ago. He was a woodsman and she was a wench.  That's really all Danny knew about her ex.

"Whoa," Stephen held up his right hand, wielding the spatula up to the heavens.  "Why do you keep calling her *Mrs. Caruso*?  Why don't you use her first name?"

Again with the spatula, Danny thought, though his face was turning red.

"She's a parent at the school.  That's what I call all the parents.  They like it when I call them Mr. and Mrs., also Ms., so don't lecture me now.  I've called her that before we started dating so it's hard to change. It's better to keep it the way it is."

Once he started talking, Danny found that it felt good to be able to order his thoughts as he spoke. His head had been so full of swirling thoughts and emotions.

"She's been married once, her ex was married once before her. He's pretty jealous, she says he drives by her house when he has custody of the kid. He's always looking for a reason to stop in and bother her. He won't accept that it's over between them, even though it's been a couple of years."

Danny felt good talking and continued. "I know it doesn't seem destined for long term success. We can't keep it secret forever. Even though we're both single, I don't think Dr. Nygren is going to appreciate one of his teachers in this situation with a parent. And twelve years is a big age gap in a relationship. And obviously, she has a child and that child has been one of my students for the past two years, that's how we met. Actually, he is the one who wrote the moon poem you liked so much, Dad. You remember, *I was making phases at the moon*."

Stephen brought Danny a cold Negra Modelo and a lime wedge and sat down next to him on the couch.

"But it's also true, that in the short run, the right now," Danny twisted off the cap and squeezed in lime juice, "we are great together. I thing we have a real strong connection and, when it's just us, it feels like we are made for each other."

Stephen tried to summarize the situation, as every father was obliged to do. "It sounds sort of like this to me, Danny. You are trying to reconcile your personal relationship with her to your professional relationship with her. Morals and ethics. It's just like the problem with reconciling the general theory of relativity, which explains gravity on the large scale, with quantum theory, which describes strong forces that act over subatomic distances and miniscule time frames."

"I don't think it's anything at all like that, Dad. Come on."

Taking that for a veiled request to continue, Stephen got up spryly and started setting the table. He spun his comparison with his eyes lighting up at the most synchronous moments. He tried to stroke his recently missing beard.

"On the large scale of years and lifetimes and permanent relationships, you and Mrs. Caruso have some challenges." Placemats. "But on the small scale of short time frames, those hours that you hide away together, and at extremely close distances, you make perfect sense together." Napkins, forks. "So when you get to spend time together, you create a relationship bubble, three or four hours long, and you can let your emotions and feelings flow." Knives and spoons. "Inside the relationship bubble, you and she are very close together and experience the strong forces of attraction. But the bubble is inevitably burst by time. Then it's back to the regular world, the larger world dominated by gravity, where you two are back to your challenges." Glasses.

The timer rang and Stephen turned to the oven. Danny stood up quickly to save the old man's knee.

"I'll get those from the oven, Dad, have a seat. It's all about physics, huh? But I stand by what I said, no, I don't think it's anything at all like that."

They sat down at the dinner table and served their plates. Stephen rallied as only he could, digging into his stacked tortillas, "So, tell me something nice about her."

Danny knew what his father meant; he wasn't questioning whether he could name something nice, he was really asking to learn something about her. Danny thought about the weekend before when they were shopping in an antique store (her idea) with Eric (again, her idea).

*We were walking through the store when Eric ran up to a lamp and pointed for his mom to look. "Mom, this lamp is just like the one we have at home!"*

*It looked like something from the 60's or 70's. Its shape was like a genie bottle. The lower part of the bottle was decorated like a beige globe. There were small shapes cut out of the oceans but they didn't match the shapes of the real oceans. It tapered up in its beigeness to the lightbulb socket.*

*She said to Eric, "Yes, it's just like the one at home." She and her ex had divided their furniture and she had kept the lamp. She liked it because it reminded her of when she bought it with him. He had wanted it, but she kept it in her side of the tradeoffs and she always felt a little bad about that.*

*"Eric, let's get it."*

*"Why? We already have one like it."*

*"We can give it to Daddy as a present. He likes lamps." And maybe he will mellow out, she hoped.*

*When she checked out, she declined their offer to ship it for her. While I was carrying it out of the store, I asked, "Why don't you just ship it to him directly?"*

*She waited two beats, almost three, when she finally answered, "I'll keep this one. I'll send him the real one. I'll tell him the one I'm sending is an exact match that I'd seen antiquing and thought he might like even if it was a copy."*

*I thought that was very nice.*

Stephen broke my silence. "Well, are you going to tell me?"

"Dad, it has something to do with lamps, but I really don't think that's the point. She is a very nice person."

"One last bit of fatherly advice. First get me a beer."

When Danny had spared his father's knee a trip to the refrigerator, Stephen dispensed his advice. "Being in a relationship is like being on a couch. You can be asleep, you can slouch, or you can sit on the edge and pay attention."

After dessert, Stephen walked Danny to the door. Danny pointed to the replica of Hammurabi's code standing on the mantle. It had several large cracks in it.

"I haven't seen this one here before," Danny asked. "What is it?"

"It's one of the oldest codes of laws in the world. Hammurabi's code."

"Ah, I've heard of it," said Danny.

"I just learned some stuff about him.  He was a Babylonian king about 3,800 years ago.  He got the law straight from the mouth from Shamash, the Babylonian god of justice.  Law 196 says *If a man destroy the eye of another man, they shall destroy his eye.*"

"It looks like it got *smashed* in transit, it's got huge cracks in it."

Stephen stepped backward happily, with wide eyes, knowing that he had to return a pun with a pun. "Believe me, when I saw the cracks in it when it arrived, I emailed the eBay seller to see who broke the law!"

## Chapter A

I knew the location of *Hawk's Gun and Archery Range,* but I hadn't been out that way in years, it was on the other side of Clayton.  When I last saw it, it was a golf range.  My client told me her brother goes to the range to blow off steam Wednesdays at ten.  I thought it a little odd that a soldier coping with PTSD would choose a gun range to relax but everyone is different.

I waited in my car until I saw his Uber come into the parking lot.  I got out and approached him as he neared the entrance.  I introduced myself, showed him my ID, and told him that his sister had asked me to talk to him.  I didn't expect him to be happy to see me.  For once, I was right.

"I'm going to get your dealer from the *Flat Fifth* busted," I told him.  "Your sister is worried you'll just find another dealer."

"What gives you the right to mess around in my life?" he said angrily, predictably.

"I'm worried more about your sister, she's my client. This time she came to me to help you, I'm not sure what she will do the next time." Play the little sister card.

"It's none of her business, I can take care of myself." He was getter angrier.

"I was in the first Gulf War, I know a little bit about what you're dealing with," I said. "I sat in a tent in Kuwait for two months waiting and then did cleanup behind burned out tanks with what was left of Republican Guards. It's not what I expected to see when I went over there." Play the vet card.

"You don't know shit about me."

I looked around the range. "This place looks pretty expensive. How can you afford it?" Play the change the subject card.

"Vets get full use of all facilities once a week for two hours for free. The owners know we need a place to be alone and not be bothered," he glared up at me.

"Well, I told her I would talk to you. Here's a card for a rehab place downtown that I know has worked for other vets. For her sake, why don't you give it a try." Play the rehab card card.

He took the card and told me to try a biological activity on myself that I have to admit I'd thought of in the past. I turned away before he could get a victory by throwing it on the ground in front of me.

## Chapter B

The drone salesman parked his pickup in the pasture of the blueberry farm.  As he walked up to the carport where the blueberry business was conducted, he passed two signs saying: "This is a Garden of Eden, Not a Garden of Eatin'" and "This is a You Pick It, not a You Eat It".  He saw his potential customer, Tess Gengler, standing under the carport roof.  She was wearing her bee-keeping safety equipment so he couldn't see her face, but he assumed it was her.  Her black lab was lying on the ground fast asleep, breathing at the top of her lungs.

When she saw him approach, she unzipped the head protection and said hello.

"Hi, are you Justin?"

Justin gave his salesman smile and said, "Yes.  You must be Tess?  Nice to meet you."

"Just give me a minute to change out of this bee stuff and I'll be right back." She walked inside the house connected to the carport.

"Great," Justin said, "I'll set up the drone."

When she came back out, she was carrying a small gun in one hand and a flare in the other. She had on safety glasses.

In response to the quizzical look on his face, she gave a smile as she said, "Don't worry. I just need to scare away the birds from the field."

As she walked to the front of the blueberry field, the dog rose and followed expectantly, knowing what was coming. When she got to the edge of the field, she put the cap ammo under the hammer and the flare into the muzzle. She pointed the gun at the middle of the field, turned her head away, closed her eyes, and fired. The flare went screaming across the field and the birds scattered. The dog ran into the field, chasing birds, and sniffing for the spent flare. Tess yelled, "Go birds go!" and clapped her hands.

After a minute or two, Tess and the dog came back to the carport and she returned the flare gun to the house. The dog had the spent flare in her mouth and didn't look like she was going to give it up anytime soon.

Justin asked, "How often do you have to do that?  Do the neighbors ever complain?"

"I shoot it about twice a day during berry season, in the morning and the evening.  I can't stand to see those birds just chomping away at the crop.  As for the neighbors," she pointed her head in the direction of the neighborhood adjoining the farm, "we were here first.  They should consider the flare as a sign that the picking season is about to start."

The salesman sensed his opportunity.  "Let's see how the *Hawk* can help."  He'd prepared to show her how the drone could help her monitor the fields, but the bird management seemed just as important to her.

"Are you looking forward to a good crop this year?" he asked as he configured the drone with additional sounds.

"I sure hope so," she replied, "if these darn birds don't get it all. Last year would have been good but we had a few spells of Old Testament weather that did in most of the crop. This year, I hope I can get most of my money back out of it."

The drone was ready now, idling more or less at her eye level, about twenty feet away. The four-legged drone hovered, whirling blades, awaiting commands.

"We're ready now," the Hawk salesman said looking at his phone. "It's all controlled through your phone." He smiled at the farmer and held out the phone for her to see.

"Look, you can tell it do almost anything you want. This button tells the drone to fly along the farm boundary and transmit the pictures beneath it to the phone. You can see which rows have the most crop, which plants need help. You can save all the video on the cloud." The drone took off and headed for the field of fruit.

Her dog lay on the ground obediently, paws out front, staring at the stranger, waiting for a command to bark or drive him away.

The salesman said, "That's a pretty serious looking dog!"

Tess replied, "I hardly ever see her smile." She wanted the dog to be imposing and it took a lot of training to get her this way.

He held the phone out for her to push the red button on the app. She poked the button like she was pruning one of her blueberry bushes. The phone immediately showed the pasture as the drone flew over the bushes and headed for the farm's border with the subdivision's walking trail. The drone issued a loud screech and the salesman smiled.

"That's authentic, too," Justin bragged. "It's a real recording of a red tailed hawk. Those robins will think twice about eating your crop with this flying around. I only installed hawk sounds because the model is called the

Hawk, but I think we can get about ten more predator sounds that should scare off your free loaders."

Behind the carport, Tess could hear her chickens scamper back to their coop, hopping and clucking trying to evade the hawk sound, recorded or not.

"Hmm," Tess said. "Could you also put something on the bottom of it so that it gives the shadow of a hawk? That would scare the little darlings even more."

Justin laughed. The birds were definitely the key to this sale. "Absolutely. Just remember that you can also fly this baby above your crops and see exactly where the problems are. Not that your crops have any problems, you understand," he apologized with a salesman smile.

She shook her head and said, "I wonder what my mother would have said about this! Probably something like, *Lord, they're growing drones on the farm now.*" Tess was wondering if she really afford a drone anyway? How is it going to pay for itself? – the existential question every farm purchase had to answer.

She looked at the screen and asked him to make the drone fly lower so she could see the field in more detail. "Can you make it fly over a couple of the blueberry rows and we can see if it really will keep away the birds? Then for sure you'd have a sale," she laugh-talked to him.

She has a beautiful smile, he thought. It hit him like a sudden short spring shower.

"Sure, it can fly in circles over the crops and make random loud noises – I've been accused of that myself!" He bent his eyes onto the app and tried to see her reaction with his peripheral vision. He kept his official smile on his face.

"Before that, I'll do you even one better. I'll put this baby on infrared mode and you can see if any raccoons or possums are hiding in the woods on the edge of the fields."

With the drone camera in infrared mode, the screen turned to greens and yellows and blues as the drone slowly made a bee line to the edge of the tree buffer and the walking trail. He was navigating the drone back to the blueberry rows when he suddenly stopped it. "Oh my God," he said. He tapped furiously as he maneuvered the drone back to the tree line near the walking path. He put the camera on rotate to get a wider view.

"There!" He paused the drone and stared again at the picture.

Tess said, "What is it?" and craned her neck at the phone only to see a red outline of a man lying on the ground.

# Chapter C

On Friday morning, that scumbag's murder was all over the local newspaper websites. I recognized his smiling face and shock of white hair in the News and Observer article. Detective Lewis Roberts was in charge of the case and was asking the public for information on the victim.

I was going to have to go to police headquarters a little sooner than I had planned. I knew Roberts and I would tell him what I knew and give him the pictures of the drug buys at the *Flat Fifth*. I would try to keep my client out of it as long as I could. And her brother.

I looked out the high window one more time, through the manzanita and eucalyptus leaves, just to ensure that no dangerous dames were staking out the plaza – public safety is my motto. I wasn't sure if I'd take a yellow bike or a lime bike to police headquarters – there was mystery even in *my* life.

# Chapter D

<u>Memorandum – Summary of Case RPA-238: Murder of Grafe, PJ</u>

<u>Written by:</u> Investigating Officer, Detective Sergeant Lewis Roberts, Durham Police Department

1) Search of victim's house (1961 Mammoth Drive, Durham) discovered the following:

   - A burner cell phone with several incoming and outgoing calls (numbers are being traced but initial results show that most numbers were also anonymous burner phones)
     - Victim's administrative assistant was unaware of the victim's burner phone.
   - Victim's company-supplied cell phone with approximately 50 contacts (numbers are being traced)
   - No indication of expensive items beyond the means of the victim's salary at Ptolemy Institutional Review Board

2) Warrants on victim's financial records should yield results in the next two days

3) Results of interviewing co-workers at Ptolemy (signed statements pending)

- Administrative assistant mentioned only one problem in the workplace. Victim had recently deferred consideration on a clinical trial submission and the principal investigator for the clinical trial, Dr. Keyen, had filed an official complaint. Dr. Keyen complained that several of his recent submissions had been either deferred or not approved and that IRB resources were being directed to clinical trials by a new pharmaceutical client that had recently starting doing business with Ptolemy. Several other clinical trials had been deferred or disapproved but those principal investigators did not file complaints.

- Members of a review board that was chaired by the victim were interviewed and stated that while the victim's deferrals and non-approvals of the clinical trials were unusual, they were not unprecedented.

- One member on the victim's review board interviewed was Stephen Yobar of Durham.  He was involved in last year's case of the attempted murder of Alexandria Knott by Dr. Arthur Moore.
  - Yobar confirms that the victim and Dr. Keyen had a bad fight at the last meeting of the review board.  When pressed, Yobar guessed that Dr. Keyen's clinical trial would likely be approved now that the victim was no longer chairing the review board.

4) Cause of death

- Initial indications were that the victim was shot with a large caliber gun but the autopsy showed that cause of death was a spear wound.  The spear had been pulled from the body (presumably by the killer) and left a large hole in the victim's chest.  The body had been dragged into the woods.

A search of the area did not discover the spear or any footprints in the vicinity of where the spear could have been thrown or shot. The victim also suffered a perimortem blow to the head with a blunt instrument (stone) but that was not the cause of death.

- Due to the disturbance of the body, it wasn't possible to calculate the trajectory of the spear so the search area will be enlarged.

5) Next steps

- Investigate the relationship between the victim and the new pharmaceutical client to determine why the victim approved clinical trials from the pharmaceutical company and did not approve other clinical trials like those of Dr. Keyen

- Cross-reference financial dealings from victim's bank records with the phone numbers found on the victim's company phone and burner phone

- Request copies of all the victim's recent activity at Ptolemy IRB and review them with Stephen Yobar

- The earliest lead so far are the photos of the victim dealing drugs at the *Flat Fifth* supplied by a private detective.  Durham detectives are following up at the music club to identify the other people in the photos with Grafe. Narcotics will give us what they have on the *Flat Fifth*.

## Chapter E

Early Monday morning, Merrimac rode her bike to the farm. She took the American Tobacco Trail to the Mammoth subdivision and then cut through the back to Tess' farm. She'd just gotten back from a monitoring trip and so she was taking today as comp time. She never would have believed that she would spend a day off taking care of bees, but then again she never thought she would be dating someone like Stephen either. Even though they were in the same general occupational area (clinical trials), he was so unlike anyone else she had ever dated: he was a few years older, he was a bit off, he had backyard chickens, and he had a son about ten years younger than she was.

When she got to the farm carport, Tess was there and they exchanged hugs.

"Here's your new bee suit," Tess said as she handed it to Merrimac. "Make sure that all the zippers are tight. The bees aren't going to be too happy with our inspections today."

"You seem pretty happy, though," Merrimac noticed. "Anything new going on?" She smiled at Tess.

"Well, I'm thinking of getting a drone to drive the birds away," Tess replied. "That makes me pretty happy." And the drone salesman is coming by later, she thought but didn't add aloud.

When they were both suited up, they walked towards the beehives with the dog in tow. They stopped at a barn and got a wagon that had the bee keeping supplies. They pulled the wagon past the bee fields[11] and got to the five beehives. Each hive had three boxes and was perched on

---

[11]

The crescent of miniature daisies,
"Frost aster" to botanists and their friends,
Covered with small butterflies and wee moths.
They hop and jump as we walk by
They flit and flat and barely fly.

a scale.  The hives were named for famous queens: Victoria, Elizabeth, Latifah, Cleopatra, and Selene.  The dog laid down under an oak tree well away from the bee hives, having learned her bee lessons.

"Merri, can you record the weights of the hives?  I hope they're filling up with honey.  After that, I'll start taking off the top boxes and see if there are any new baby cells.  I've got a feeling that Cleopatra is about to swarm."  Tess started the smoker, a metal container holding pine needles that she lit.  She would pump smoke onto the bees so they would move and not get crushed when she put the box back in its place.  Inevitably, a few bees always did get crushed.  Merrimac was upset the first time she saw it happen so Tess told her, "If you can't take killing a few baby bees by inspecting the hives, you're in the wrong business."

"First, we need to see if they need food."  Tess looked at the weights that Merrimac had just transcribed into the bee notebook.  "Hmm.  A couple seem a little light, they must be eating their honey.  I'll mix a few gallons of sugar water and we can pour some in the top of the light hives.

While I'm doing that, can you walk from here to over past the Mammoth Way path and see if there is anything still in bloom? The pollen plants here have gone to seed."

This is a pretty great job, Merrimac thought, walking around the farm looking for wildflowers. So much better than walking through airports hoping to get into the fastest security line.

When she got near the Mammoth Way path, there was still yellow tape in the woods marking the spot where the body was found. She avoided that area and kept moving towards the walking path. She took photos of all the flowers that were blooming and tried to remember if they had pollen or nectar.

As the trees thinned, there was tall grass and wildflowers all the last six feet to the walking path. At the edge of the tree line, she saw tall stand of purple and pink wildflowers in amongst the browning clover. She took some extra close-up pictures to identify the flowers and see if they were bee-friendly. She crossed the path and took more photos of the flowers on that side. After a few

more minutes, she returned to the bee hives.  She could
smell the burning pine needles as she approached.

# Chapter F

Detective Roberts asked Stephen to come to headquarters to help with some questions about the IRB and the clinical trials that Grafe had rebuffed. Roberts had reviewed the trials that had been rejected or hurt by Grafe's decisions, but they didn't mean much to him so he wanted Stephen's input. There were a variety of investigators affected by Grafe's decisions, but only a few who had been hit hard.

Roberts had Ptolemy IRB send him summaries of all Grafe's clinical trials and to highlight the six that were fast-tracked by Grafe in the past year. Those all involved Simon and Angelo Pharmaceuticals, a relatively small company in RTP. Per their website, SAP made drugs to treat opiate addicts, specifically vets who were suffering from post-traumatic stress disorder. Once the vets were off the opiates, the SAP drugs for PTSD could be used to treat the vets. Roberts was particularly interested in a report written by Grafe when he performed an on-site audit of the SAP facility. Per the report, Grafe initiated the audit because SAP was one of the few sponsors that Ptolemy supported where illegal opiates were expected to be used because many of the volunteer subjects were addicts. Also, SAP's anti-opiate drug was developed from opiates so their process was tightly controlled by the Food and Drug Administration. Roberts thought there was a link between SAP and the drug dealing at the *Flat Fifth* music club but he hadn't found it yet.

Stephen read the audit report and told Roberts that an unusual goal of the clinical trial was to create a social networking map. As part of the trial, the vets would keep a diary using a phone app which recorded where and when they went to socialize. The social network could then be used by health officials to choose locations to target additional support to vets who were suffering with PTSD and who may have an opiate problem. The audit report described an appendix which wasn't initially included in the materials sent to Roberts from Ptolemy, but Stephen asked for it when he saw it referenced. Roberts got it emailed quickly to him from Ptolemy but was annoyed when Stephen asked for the appendix to be printed out.

The appendix had data on the social network created in the trial. Stephen reviewed the printouts to confirm that the subjects' identities were not included in the data; that was surely one of the first things Grafe would have done in the audit. Clinical trial subjects were identified by numeric identifiers like 100325 instead of their name or initials. According to the audit report, the link between the numeric identifier and the actual subject's identity was not kept in the same computer system as the data. The link was not included in the audit report.

However, Stephen noticed that the numeric identifiers for the locations (bars, restaurants, etc.) and their location names *could* be linked by looking at the data, which was fine from the IRB point of view. Danny started reading the locations off to Detective Roberts: the *Flat Fifth* club, the Hawk shooting range, Q Shack barbeque restaurant, Salt Box seafood restaurant downtown, and about ten more.

Stephen pointed out to Detective Roberts that even though this data wouldn't tell Grafe *who* the clinical trial subjects were, Grafe would know *where* and *when* they hung out together. Roberts figured that was enough information for Grafe to know where he could sell opiates.

"OK Stephen, that's great. But is there anything in here saying how Grafe could have gotten opiates to sell?"

Stephen looked through the audit report and saw a mention that Grafe had reviewed the inventory log at the SAP site. "Grafe could have access to the opiates listed in the SAP inventory, but those drugs are tightly controlled by the FDA," Stephen told the detective.

Roberts didn't look too happy about that. Stephen added, "Drugs used as part of clinical trials are controlled, as I said, and the regulations say that drugs that have expired can't be used in the trial because they may not be effective. It looks like the SAP inventory includes opiates, the SAP investigational anti-opiate drugs, and the SAP investigational PTSD drugs. It's possible that the person in charge of the inventory could report the expired opiates as destroyed, and still have kept them because they were probably still strong."

A theory formed in Roberts' mind: as kickback for approving clinical trials quickly, the SAP management would provide Grafe with a supply of opiates that had been reported to the FDA as expired and destroyed. Roberts finally had a link worth following up on. But what about Stephen himself?

"We'll look at the SAP people now that we've got this lead. So let's say that Grafe needed a partner at Ptolemy in his scheme. He needed someone on an ethics board to get the clinical trials approved quickly." Roberts looked coldly at Stephen.

Stephen sat there stunned.

Roberts said, "I see that you were the main reviewer of all the SAP studies that got approved quickly. Maybe you were in on it? Maybe you got a little bribe, assuming it was a cash kickback from the pharma company?"

Stephen said, "I did not! He gave me those assignments because each board member usually gets assigned similar studies over time so that they get familiar with those types of trials. PJ had me review the SAP trials because I'm non-scientist and these types of studies came down to ethics acceptable by the public. I couldn't provide any input on the medicines. There were two main ethical issues: the data privacy of the subjects and the fact that the subjects could be using the investigational anti-opiate and PTSD drugs while still using illegal opiates which could cause serious adverse events."

Roberts used his typical tactic of keeping quiet to see what Stephen would say.

"In my review of this study, I looked at how the clinical trial data was going to be stored," Stephen continued when Roberts' silence got uncomfortable. "Remember those numeric codes for the subjects? In my review, I thought their procedures protected subjects' privacy. The link between the code numbers and the subjects' real names weren't even stored on the same computer network, so even if the network were hacked, the identities would still be protected. That's just what Grafe confirmed in this report. The benefits of the study outweighed the risks, I felt, and that the volunteer subjects also had the potential to benefit from the research. That's why I recommended to the board that the study be approved. Not any kickbacks!"

Roberts nodded and said, "How about this then? You found out he was dealing drugs to vets and you decided to deal out some justice yourself. Law of the jungle, is that why you used a spear? And that atlatl thing to throw it? And why did you bash his skull afterwards?"

Stephen sat in silence. The detective grinned and said, "No, I don't think you did it. But I had to ask."

Roberts drank some coffee. "Do you think anyone else in the Ptolemy corporate group or on the ethics board could have been cahooting with Grafe? Or willing to kill him if they had found out?"

"I have no idea," Stephen answered. "I can't think of one person."

"All right, you can go," Roberts said and stood up. "Thanks for your help."

As Stephen got to the office door, Roberts said, "Don't leave town without letting me know."

Stephen looked back with shock at Roberts.

"Just kidding.  You always seem to be the one joking so I thought you could take it.  Actually, there is something you can help with if you can.  I think it's time to stir the pot."

# Chapter 10

After Stephen's questioning by Detective Roberts, and realizing that Grafe was murdered near the farm where Merrimac volunteered, he definitely wanted to survey the scene. Merrimac agreed but she said they couldn't go on the farm itself unless they had permission from Tess, the owner, which Merrimac asked for and then received.

They drove to the Mammoth neighborhood and parked close to the walking path. They crossed some grass and then over the walking path into a wooded area. About ten feet into the wooded area, and on the right, police tape still surrounded the location where the body was found. They walked through the woods and stopped at the farm pasture. This area of the farm had beehives and fields of clover.

Stephen noticed lines[12] under patches of pasture dirt and wondered to Merrimac what they were. Merrimac said that Tess had mentioned that they were underground pipes to fill the ponds back when they had cows.

Merrimac turned to him and asked, "Do you hear that noise? Like a meow?"

Stephen pointed to a branch in the large tree. "It's not a cat, it's that squirrel on that branch!"

"Why is it making that noise?"

"Maybe the squirrel is trying to impersonate a cat," Stephen guessed.

"Why?" she asked.

"To attract acorns. Why else would a squirrel do anything?"

---

[12]

You read my patterns, like scars on the pasture,
You see my reasons known and half-known
As I flux from man to animal to man.
You sigh when you see
The pasture hearth beneath the June moon,
Me howling like a solstice loon.

She smiled and then was quiet for a few moments to let that pass. "What kind of guy are you?" she asked looking at the pasture, then at Stephen. She thought that was one of the nice things about him, you could ask him open-ended questions and it didn't throw him off.

"Well... I'm not the type who mopes around reciting poems to myself, if that's what you think.[13]"

That's exactly what I think, she thought. "I don't think that," she said.

Stephen said, "I've got a question for you. Why do you like coming to this farm and volunteering? It sounds like a lot of work."

"Working with the bees and crops is a nice break from the office and traveling," Merrimac explained. "Plus, I

---

[13]

Blue haired
Blonde eyed,
Dutch by way of Des Moines.
She was a love bubble of
Space time energy beauty.
My love rubbed against her,
Husks of quantum rubble
Fell at our feet.

grew up out in the boonies and it reminds me of home. We didn't have many neighbors. We had a hill behind our house that ran down to the creek. My sisters and I would cross the creek and go up the hill and play in the woods. We didn't know where the property lines were, it didn't matter."

"That sounds like a great place to play," Stephen agreed softly.

"All of us would play down in the gulley," she reminisced. "We had a great game called Gulley Rat. Whoever was down in the gulley was the Gulley Rat. The Gulley Rat would try to get out of the gulley without being tagged. The closest kid to them when they got out was then the Gulley Rat. We had a one-hill gulley for small games, and whenever we could get some friends from school to come over, we'd play two hills and that was a lot more fun." She stopped.

"I'm sure those woods are long gone by now." She turned and looked into the thin woods[14] behind her. "I guess that's why I like to come out here."

Merrimac turned to him and smiled. "Since you totally avoided my first question, I'll ask you something else. What's one of those rants that Danny is always complaining about? I want to hear one you haven't told him."

Stephen loved her smile. "I'm taking that in the best way possible, I assure you. OK. I have one about how heaven could exist."

She laughed and gave him a mock serious expression. "OK, I'm ready." She stared him in the eyes.

Stephen started. "Here's how a bubble of heaven could happen." He paused. He organized his thoughts because he know he only had one shot at this.

---

14

The shadow of a woodland elf
Bustles by, a moment out of phase,
A rustle from whispers
A blur beyond sound.

"Neutrons are made of two down quarks and one up quark. Protons have two up quarks and one down quark. The weak force, one of the four basic forces of nature in the Standard Model of physics, can, inside a neutron, mediate the change of a down quark into an up quark. This effectively turns the neutron into a proton. For good measure, this process also emits an electron to maintain electrical balance and emits quite a few little neutrinos to carry the energy that is released."

"Ah," said Merrimac. "I'm starting to see Danny's point." She sat down on the pasture and leaned back on her palms. Next time, she thought, I'll add a time limit to the rant.

But Stephen was undeterred. "Ok, here comes the heaven part.

"What would happen if you focused the weak force on densely packed neutrons, like in the atoms on this farm, and turned them into protons all at once? All those subatomic transformations would be like Cinderella's coach turning into a pumpkin."

Merrimac said, "I thought this sounded like a fairy tale."

Stephen continued. "It would release so much energy that the nearby space-time couldn't hold it (very similar to the Big Bang, but don't get me started!). So in order to accommodate that immense energy density, the farm (and you standing on it) would squirt out of our space-time universe, like a watermelon seed being shot out of a thumb and index finger. You would be in a detached bubble clinging to the outside of the universe."

Merrimac couldn't pass that one up. "Detached from the universe, you say?"

Stephen indicated by waving his arms that this was the important part. "Now that the detached bubble was out of our universe, its time would never pass, and its space would never end."

Merrimac decided to keep playing along because he looked so happy. "Hmm, never ending. I can relate to that."

Triumphantly, Stephen concluded, "With your consciousness inside that bubble, time would stand still for you. You would be able to wander infinitely in that bubble of heaven."

He waited for her to comment further, but she didn't.

At least he doesn't talk about sports all the time, she rationalized. She stood and wiped the dirt off her palms and her jeans. It was getting dark and the yellow moon was rising.[15]

Merrimac squeezed Stephen's hand and then started walking back to the car. She had finally gotten the lesson about rants that Danny was always talking about. Stephen followed happily behind her.

---

[15]

The waning moon hangs low and yellow,
Glowing Claire d'Lune dust,
Rocks turned by time into quantum rubble.

# Chapter 11

"Where'd you get that new statue?" Danny nodded his head towards a replica of a headless figure. Danny had come to his father's house before lunch to talk about his afternoon meeting with the Durham Friends School principal, Dr. Nygren.

"I bought it when I got back from the Louvre," Stephen answered. "I just put it out to go with the Hammurabi statue you liked. What do you think?"

Danny gave it a more thorough glance. "It would probably be better if it had the head."

Stephen smiled. "That reminds me of the two things I thought of the last time I was at the Louvre." One finger pointed straight up. "First, wouldn't it be great if there was a way to uniquely identify the marble statues such that the heads in, say the British Museum, could be reunited with the torsos in Greece? Identify them down to the molecular level?"

Danny debated about how to express his feelings on this issue, but was saved when Stephen continued. Two fingers pointed to the ceiling. "Second, wouldn't it be awesome if you could virtually view the missing parts of the sculptures, like the head of the Venus de Milo? And if you could see what original sculptures looked like in terms of paint and jewels?"

Danny was quick to jump on this. "That seems to go against some of your previous rants – theories, I mean – that art should be viewed as it is, not embellished?" Danny was sure he scored points with this, using his Dad's theories against him.

Stephen conceded, "True, very true, but perhaps you could view them only with special hologram or virtual reality glasses (rented for 10 euros, say), so then you would only see the Venus's head if you wanted to." He sulked for a moment, stroking his shorn beard again.

"I've got other ideas but I'll save them for later."[16]

Stephen broke out of his sulk with one of his standard questions. "So how are you really doing, Danny?" Stephen asked.

Danny didn't feel like talking about it yet so he played his dad's game.

"I feel like it's Judgement Day and I smell like lighter fluid."

Stephen laughed. "That's my boy!"

Danny recounted yesterday's conversation with Dr. Nygren. "Today is my end of year conference with Dr. Nygren. He told me yesterday that a parent had called

---

[16] The Louvre

Inscrutable igneous inscriptions
Of lives and loves long dead
Nurtured now only by the Louvre.
We imagine
Beautiful sounds,
Filled with meaning,
Tugging hearts,
Staving off our descent
Into quantum rubble.

him and complained about me dating Mrs. Caruso. Dr. Nygren felt that a teacher dating the parent of a student didn't fit in with the Quaker way. He said we would discuss it more at our end of year conference today."

"Who complained? Her ex-husband?"

"I don't know, but that's most likely. He just seems to want to cause trouble for her."

Danny paused then continued. "Dr. Nygren said that it creates the impression that I could be giving a student preferential treatment. Even worse, that I could be holding back constructive criticism of the student and that wouldn't be fair to the student. He said I was breaking the ethics of the school by being in this relationship."

"Ethics, eh? He has a point there," Stephen replied. "Is he going to give you a chance to atone for your sins?"

"I'll find out at our meeting at one," Danny replied.

Stephen said, "Who is this ex-husband anyway? That's still bugging me. Maybe if we can get into his head, we can find a way to fix this."

Danny knew this was pointless and didn't want to contradict his dad, but it did raise a question.

"This relationship stuff is crap, Dad," Danny blurted out. "You and mom seem to get along even though you're divorced.  How did that happen?"

Stephen responded, "Our marriage was like the Apollo 13 mission:  a successful failure.  You were what made it a success, Danny."

"It sounds like you still miss her a little, Dad."

"Only in a vaguely reminiscent way.  I miss her from 20 years ago, but not really now[17]."

---

17

It's not the you now that fills up my head
When I awaken and you are not here,
It's the old memories that have not yet fled
Which fade and blur and then become unclear.
Does your face still glow with the sun's first ray?
I can't remember the curve of your brow.
The you in my soul is slipping away
I'm left with an echo in a shadow.
Now I forget to remember at all,
My memories fade to quantum rubble.

Danny continued. "I always seem to say the wrong things to her.  She starts talking about the problems with her ex, and I really don't know what to say," Danny said.  "I don't want to lie or tell her something that will upset her."

"Here's the trick," Stephen counseled.  "Listen to her and tell her something true that makes her feel good instead of telling her something true that makes her feel bad."

"Maybe the problem is we're talking too much about problems," Danny suggested.  "It was more fun in the beginning when we just talked about easy things."

Stephen said, "If you don't talk about your issues, then it's like you have a rock covering up your relationship.  When you eventually do pick up the rock you see the swarming problems underneath.  That's the only way to get rid of the problems – you have to pick up the rock."

He could sense that he wasn't helping his son as much as he had hoped.  "It's all in the way you look at things,"

Stephen concluded, pointing to the blinking strands of lights that decorated his back porch. "Take those two strands of lights interlaced. Each light blinks from red to white every second. If you stare only at one light, and not at the entire display of lights, it's very boring – the light just turns from red to white and back to red. But when you look at both strands of lights together, at the overall image, then the lights interplay in ripples across the strands. It is a much more beautiful way to see the whole picture."

# Chapter 12

<u>The Drone Salesman's Dream</u>

The bark

of the frog

in the rain

up the tree

on the branch

through the fog.

Not even the frog can see

the dog sitting under the tree,

resenting fake barkers.


In my cave

in the dim dark

I have brown wood, black chairs

poorly framed images

of deeply loved ones.

On the bee farm

in a flowery embroidered dress

her name is Tess, Tess, Tess

arms laden with farm fruits:

corn in a bag, eggs in a bucket,

bees in a cup.

No one stares at pain on a farm.

# Chapter 13

Stephen and Merrimac decided to have dinner at a new place Stephen had heard about at the RTP data managers users group meeting last month. *Restaurant Pauli*, a very exclusive restaurant, had just opened where *The Boot* used to be. "It's very cozy, they only have tables for two," he told her.

The maître d' walked them to their table close to the window. "Table 1S, our best table, I hope you find it comfortable. You're lucky to get that table, it fills up fast." Stephen asked if he could sit on the same side as Merrimac but the maître d' told him no[18].

---

[18]

We shared an orbital, snug and in love
I shared all my quantum numbers with you.
Pauli said one of us would have to go!
After one last look into your soft eyes
I jumped to a new, lonely orbital
Empty with nothing but quantum rubble.

Stephen was a little shocked, "Why? Is it against the rules?"

The waiter responded, "No, it's not a rule, it's more like it's against our principles of dining." He took their drink order and disappeared.

In a few minutes, the waiter reappeared with two glasses of wine.

Merrimac pointed towards the back of the restaurant. "This table is nice but the ones at the back have those wild lights on them. It makes the people look excited."

"They look a little out of their element, if you ask me," Stephen said of the young group she was referring to.

"So, what have you thinking about lately?" Merrimac asked him a little uncertainly, taking a sip of her wine.

Stephen thought for a moment before he answered. He decided on a poem from the Wallace Stevens book they got in Raleigh, *Thirteen ways of looking at a blackbird*. He quoted:

*"He rode over Connecticut in a glass coach.*

*Once a fear pierced him in that he mistook the shadow of his equipage for blackbirds."*

"I can never keep that straight, *rode over* or *rode across*," she said frustratedly.

Stephen offered, "I think of it not in the context of the line, but just those two words. *Rode over* sounds more old school, *across* is a newfangled word."

"What does that even mean, *in a glass coach*?" She took another sip of wine.

"I've always thought of the blackbirds as a positive image in the different stanzas of the poem," Stephen continued as he drank from his glass. "But some of the poems have something good that is suddenly upset by the blackbirds."

Merrimac offered, "Oh, so like it could represent death, something bad."

As Merrimac's words reverberated in his mind, Stephen's eyes opened wide. "Oh my God, I can't believe I never thought of the poem like this before! *He rode over*

*Connecticut in a glass coach.* I had always imagined an 18th century horse-drawn coach going down a road. But the glass coach is really his body! And the next line - *Once a fear pierced him in that he mistook the shadow of his equipage for blackbirds.* I just thought that was the shadow of his horses and their harness equipment." Stephen sipped his wine.

"But with your new theory, Merrimac, it makes much more sense. The *glass coach* is his body, so the glass coach is riding over Connecticut just like his body is living in Connecticut. Out of the corner of his eyes he sees the shadow of blackbirds, but what he's really seeing out of the corner of his eyes is time and entropy masquerading as death. So the shadow he sees is death lurking behind his body. We all live in denial of the death that follows us as certainly as our own shadow follows us."

Merrimac didn't want to ruin his moment. "I don't think that's exactly my new theory, but I'll take a win when I can get one."

## Chapter 14

Stephen parked outside of SAP's building in Morrisville. It was about three miles from Alexandria Knott's *We Do Monitoring* clinical research organization; he would stop by and hello to her when he was finished here.  Merrimac was offsite doing an audit today.  He hadn't seen Alexandria since she got out of the hospital.  She was now recovered from the poisoning and was working hard on the HIV vaccine with AMP, Arthur Moore Pharmaceutical minus the now deceased Arthur Moore.  He didn't know if AMP had rebranded, but he figured it was better to google it than to ask Alexandria.

At the receptionist's desk, he checked in while he saying he was here for a meeting with Timothy Simon. "He'll be down in a moment," the receptionist said and he gave Stephen a visitor's pass.  Simon arrived a minute later and said, "Thanks, Phil," to the receptionist and he led Stephen to his office.

Simon was about five feet ten inches, mid-forties, and in much better shape that Stephen. He was probably considered handsome if you happened to like thin men with nice professional smiles. In Stephen's estimation, the only that that he had going on better than Simon was his hair; Simon's was thinning and Stephen's was still a force to be reckoned with. Simon invited Stephen to sit in the visitor's chair in his office.

Stephen declined an offer of pod brewed coffee.

When Simon sat down, he said, "How can I help you, Stephen?" He had the audit email from Ptolemy IRB open on his computer. It said that it was time for another audit of their two clinical trials on PTSD in veterans, but Ptolemy had never audited them two times so close together. He recognized Stephen's name from the documentation that the IRB sent previously on the initial approvals of his studies and the periodic approvals to keep the studies going.

"As you probably have heard," Stephen began, "PJ Grafe, who did the previous audits, was killed two weeks ago."

Simon furrowed his brow and replied, "Yes, I heard, that was pretty awful. I worked with him a few times here on the audits."

Stephen nodded and continued. "PJ had made me the primary reviewer on all SAP trials. He trusted my speedy reviews on the trials and he had been giving me, let's say, cash bonuses to get the trials approved initially and to ensure that the continuing reviews of the trials resulted in approvals. He was very concerned that your research continue without interruption. As part of the distribution of his responsibilities, the executive committee has assigned me the entire SAP portfolio."

Simon didn't reply, but began to organize a few papers on his desk.

"After what happened to PJ, Ptolemy initially wanted to slow down on all trials that PJ was managing, just to make sure nothing is wrong. Now that I'm the SAP portfolio manager, I was able to convince the executive committee that slowing down your trials isn't necessary. I said that my doing another audit would be sufficient and a wise move considering the sensitive nature of your studies, especially with the involvement of opiates."

Stephen let that last word hang in the air and decided not to say anything more until Simon replied. Simon was better at this than Stephen was and so he was forced to continued anyway. "According to the last audit, it looks like you have two batches of opiates about to expire and be destroyed next week. PJ was the witness on the FDA forms for several previous destructions so I think I could be the witness on this next destruction of opiates. PJ explained the entire process to me." Stephen lifted his eyebrows as he said *process*. "Maybe we could get a head start on it today."

Simon turned to his computer and pulled up the opiate supply list in Excel and looked at the lot expiration dates. "It looks like we destroyed lot 49 two days ago, but lot 50 is set to expire next week, you're right." He swiveled back to Stephen, looked him in the eye, and said, "No use crying about lot 49, but I'll need to talk to my partner about the timing of the destruction of lot 50. Let me get back to you in a couple days and we can arrange an appointment."

Stephen summed up. "I know you had a good relationship with PJ and I think things could continue that way with me as the new portfolio manager. These clinical trials are important and I wouldn't want to see them stopped."

Simon issued his own admonition. "I explained to PJ several times that in the pharma trade, you can't get too greedy. Once a deal is made, you have to stick with it. We're all in this together for the science."

Stephen agreed. "PJ did have a bit of a reputation for being greedy at Ptolemy, but I'm not that way. Once a deal is made, I stick with it. I'm involved in more studies than PJ was. I'm also the portfolio manager for trials Ptolemy approves in nursing homes and homeless shelters. Those people need our support too."

Simon stood up and walked Stephen back to the receptionist's desk and shook his hand goodbye. "Make sure you get the visitor's pass back, Phil. We want to make sure our logs look good for our next audit."

# Chapter 15

Not many years ago, the idea of sitting by the pool having a drink in downtown Durham was unthinkable. But the *Unscripted Hotel* changed that. The five story hotel sat in the middle of the new thriving downtown, with a full view of the Bull Statue plaza. The cobalt blue and white hotel had a *serve your own beer* store on one end of the ground floor and a Mediterranean restaurant at the other end. The pool was on the second floor so Ann walked through the lobby (with a bar of its own) and took the elevator up one floor to see her friend for a poolside drink. Ann had just finished teaching her Friday afternoon cooking class for teenagers at the Durham Arts Council a few blocks away and was thirsty herself after walking in the late afternoon June sun.

The pool area was about half-full, not bad for Friday at 4. A few small groups were in the pool hitting around some oversized beach balls. Electronic house music blared out, perhaps trying a bit too hard for this early in the weekend. Ann stopped by the bar and ordered an old fashioned and then sat under the umbrella where Mrs. Caruso had saved a place for her.

"Thanks," Ann said to the bartender as he delivered her drink a short minute later. Mrs. Caruso asked for a refill on her wine which was half gone.

"Wow, this is really nice," Ann said. "Lounging poolside with a drink. Great start to the weekend." She smiled and clinked glasses with her friend. "We're relaxing and the kids are where they belong – with their fathers!"

"You're lucky with your husband," Mrs. Caruso.

"Thomas works at home most of the time these days, he only has to go to Atlanta about once a month," Ann agreed. "It's nice that I can count on him when I'm working late on proposals, which seems like more and more even though I'm half-time." She was careful not to go on too much about her good situation when her friend was having rough times with her ex, which seemed like all the time lately.

Mrs. Caruso took a drink of her wine and complimented her friend. "That's a cute dress." Ann's dress was summery, but a little too short so she was wearing some black leggings with a purple pattern underneath.

"It's putting me in the vacation mood," Ann replied and took a small sip of her excellent old fashioned.

Mrs. Caruso asked Ann, "Any ideas where are you going to go?"

"I like the mountains more than the beach, especially at this time of year," Ann mused. "Thomas doesn't really have a preference, as long as the Wi-Fi is good enough for him to work. I'm looking for a medium-sized hike to a waterfall, Lara likes to hike. Or at least she doesn't complain too much on our hikes through Umstead."

She looked through her sunglasses at Mrs. Caruso. "What about you and Eric? Any plans?"

Mrs. Caruso reached for her glass of wine. "I'm not thinking about vacations any time soon. Eric told me that he and his dad drove by one evening recently when Danny was over. It wasn't much longer until someone complained to Danny's principal about our relationship." She took two sips. "If he's going to start doing crap like that, I don't know what I'm going to have to do." Another sip. "So I haven't had time to cook up vacation plans."

"Eric could sign up for a music camp," Anny offered. "I got an email saying that UNC had slots available in July for their beginning music camp, one week long. Eric seems to like it when I play the piano when I watch him, especially the boogie woogie. He loves to sing. I bet he's a natural for the bass." She smiled and said, "Hey, maybe Lara and I should sign up too and we could make a band!"

Mrs. Caruso was uplifted for a moment. "That sounds like fun! Danny likes playing in his band." After mentioning Danny's name, her face became a little crestfallen. She took the last sip of wine. Where was the bartender with her refill?

"Danny. I don't think that's going to last much longer. He got in pretty bad trouble at school and it's hard for that not to put a strain on our relationship, especially when it's my fault because of my ex." She looked relieved when the bartender approached balancing her new glass of wine on the circular cork carrying tray. "Sometimes I think it would be easier to just move away."

"Where would you go?" Ann asked concernedly.

"I'm not sure. Far away from that jerk as I can; it's in our agreement that I can move out of state. But it needs to be in an area with good hospitals because of Eric's blood disorder that needs monitoring. It doesn't bother him much as you know. The hospitals here made this a great location for Eric but…"

Ann didn't like to think of her good friend moving away, and Lara and Eric were becoming good friends too.

"Let's just relax for the evening," Ann decided. "I'll text Thomas that we're having dinner downtown. We can finish our drinks and people watch for a while. We can eat at *Nana Steak* or something like that. And when we can get that bartender's attention again, we'll get another round and ask him to turn down the volume, or at least point that speaker away."

# Chapter 16

In the parking lot off Anderson Street, Stephen sat in his car and looked at the text from Merrimac again. "At 10 in Duke Gardens come back and see, the place where we wanted to drink some tea." He sighed, but in a good way. Merrimac had some friends that she went to a puzzle room with once or twice a year, so he shouldn't have been surprised that she wanted to play a puzzle room game with him. The first clue was the text this morning.

He walked through the Duke Gardens front entrance and passed the info center/canteen. You could probably buy tea there, but that isn't what Merrimac meant. He remembered that they walked through the Asian gardens before and sat outside a secluded building that looked like an old Japanese tea room. It had been closed at the time, but it was a beautiful spot.

The entrance to the garden was spectacular with a great view down the thirty-foot wide steps to a huge fountain in the center of a roundabout walking path. The magnolia trees were blooming in June, but it was nothing like the scene six weeks earlier at Easter when the flowers were in full bloom. On the plus side, it was easier to park now and the garden wasn't as jammed with people.

Stephen walked down the grand stairway and turned right, following the signs to the Japanese gardens. The centerpiece was a large pond filled with koi fish. He crossed the red bridge and made an immediate left towards the tea house. The tea house was closed again ("Open from 10-12, Tuesdays and Thursdays") so he sat on the same bench where Merrimac had sat with him on their previous visit.

He looked around for a clue but didn't see one. I'd probably be stuck in one of those puzzle rooms all night if I went in, he thought. After a moment, he got down (slowly) onto both knees and looked under the bench. An envelope was duck taped to the underside of the bench. He removed it and eased his way back onto the bench, slightly rubbing his left knee. Inside there was a card that said, "We had a kiss and emotions flowed, in the beautiful spot where time slowed."

It had to mean the old sun dial they had found when looking for a place to rest last time. It was down further into the gardens. Stephen walked back to the pond and headed to the main garden path. On his right, a huge open lawn was full of kids and adults playing and sitting on blankets. In one group of kids, a boy was shouting, "Quien es, quien es alta?" A girl of about 10 responded, "Estoy!" Danny played this type of game in his Spanish class with his younger students. "Quien es" means "Who is" and "Estoy" means "I am", Danny told him. In Danny's class, he said it led to more dialog. In this group, it led to more running and squeals of delight. As he kept walking down the hill, now the boy was yelling, "Quien es rapido?" No doubt the game of chase continued.

The path towards the sun dial was slightly steep and Stephen trudged down. There was a buzzing sound nearby, but he didn't see any bugs and then all of a sudden about a hundred birds started screeching in the trees. He finally looked up and saw the drone, flying twenty feet over his head, with a cardboard cutout of a hawk on the bottom. A man and a woman sitting on a blanket on the lawn were flying it, enjoying themselves. Stephen wasn't sure but it seemed like they were laughing at the birds frightful screeches.

The sun dial was on the right side of the path, he remembered when he saw the yew tree. A rock pebbled trail led him behind a bush to a bench and a sun dial. The sun dial was very cool though not very useful because the sun was blocked by the large bushes surrounding it. This time, he didn't sit on the bench, he leaned on it and groped under the seat hoping for another clue and dreading a wet piece of gum. He was rewarded with the former.

"You've made it this far I give you no fake'ry, Meet me at six at the underground bakery."

Two months ago, Stephen would have thought, why couldn't she just ask me to meet her at the bakery at six? But he kept learning more about Merrimac and he was happy as he walked back to the parking lot.

At six o'clock, Stephen walked into the "The Boss's Bassett Underground Bakery" and joined Merrimac at her seat by the window. She beamed a smile at him. "Wasn't Duke Gardens as least fun as the great gift card chase you took me on?"

As Stephen was about to say yes, she added, "And how about my awesome poem clues? You're starting to have a bad influence on me." She laughed and gave him a quick kiss.

After getting their coffee and a slice of pie, Stephen was quiet for almost two minutes, a phenomenon that Merrimac had rarely experienced.

"What's wrong?" she asked with a concerned look.

Stephen sighed and answered, "Danny called me last night. The police got a tip that the weapon that killed PJ Grafe was in Danny's car. Detective Roberts asked him if he could search Danny's car and of course he said yes. The spear that killed Grafe, along with some kind of spear launcher, and a stone that the killer used to hit Grafe in the head, were all in the trunk."

"That's horrible," Merrimac's eyes widened.

"I called Roberts this morning and he said he really doesn't suspect Danny, but that maybe someone is trying to get back at me for something I did for Roberts."

"What? What did you do for the police?" Now Merrimac was getting more upset.

"Detective Roberts asked for some help with the case because I know about some of the clinical trials at Ptolemy that Grafe was involved in. I said yes, but now I'm starting to regret it. Danny's name was in the newspapers with mine because of the Alexandria Knott thing so he's an easy target." Stephen sat quietly again. "Let's change the subject."

Merrimac turned on her iPad and showed Stephen the pictures she took of the wildflowers at Tess's farm earlier that week. She magnified and cropped the pictures so that she could post them on Facebook and ask the plant identification group to identify the species. Once identified, she could google the wildflower names and see if they were good for bees. Tess would be very happy to see the results.  As she magnified one of the images, she noticed something strange lying on top of a flower at the tree line.  It looked like a small circular stone with a hole for a necklace string.  From its location off the side of the Mammoth Way path, it could be where the murder happened, they decided.  Maybe it was nothing but maybe it was a clue to the murder and to who had tried to frame Danny.

"Let's go back and find that stone." she said.  "Maybe it can help."

She drove them to the Mammoth Way development and parked near the walking path. She walked them to the spot on Mammoth Way path where she had photographed the flowers and the stone. With the wind blowing towards them, Stephen could almost smell the honey from the hives[19].

She found the exact spot of the where the stone should be by lining up with a bush and the trees that were in the background of the photo. She and Stephen both looked for a half hour through the flowers, in ever widening circles, but it was gone.

---

[19]

Night falling slow on a Midsummer's eve
Honey bees lounging on their beehive porch
Tall wildflowers, drained of Spring's colors,
Play hide and seek at dusk with fireflies.
Are their lights magic or just chemistry?
Fireflies appearing, disappearing,
Reappearing moments later nearby
Hopscotching in and out of orbitals
Leaving behind a yellow afterglow
Of softly shimmering quantum rubble.

# Chapter 17

Thanks for coming in again.

My pleasure, Detective Roberts.  Always grateful for the opportunity to assist the police in their enquiries.

Those pictures you had of Grafe selling pills at the *Flat Fifth* were very useful.  You have my thanks.

He nodded and put the verbal IOU in his pocket.

Those were all the pictures you had, correct?

I'll double check my records, but I think so.

OK.  Do you know who Danny Yobar is?

The name rings a bell.

Last year he was involved with the Alexandria Knott case.

Ah, yes, now I remember.  He claimed that he was standing on the road by his sabotaged car when a pharmaceutical company CEO tried to run him over but the CEO got killed instead when his car hit a deer?

That's right.

And you believed it?

Sure.  You can't make that stuff up.

Why do you ask?

We're off the record now.

Silence and a nod.

We got a tip that the spear that killed Grafe was in Danny Yobar's car trunk.

Ah.  Again with the car?

Well, we asked him if we could look in the trunk and he said yes.  And sure enough, for the first time in my career, I found a spear, a stone – and I didn't make this up – a bloody atlatl in a car trunk.  We compared the stone tip on the spear to particulates on the vic's rib and it matched. The blood on the stone and atlatl was a match too.

Are you going to make me ask?

An atlatl is a wooden or bone spear thrower.  There is a notch at one end where the spear or arrow sits, and then you fling it forward.  You can put a stone on it for balance; forensics says that's how it was used before the killer hit the vic in the head with it.

Are you serious?

Google it.  The forensics team is actually having fun with this one.

What did you ask me to come in for, Detective?  It costs three bucks for the bike ride.

Still off the record.  We have a lead based on those photos you gave us.  Grafe had a pretty cozy relationship, off the books, with this pharma company, Simon and Angelo Pharmaceuticals, based in Morrisville.  They go by SAP.  They make opiate withdrawal meds and PTSD meds designed for vets and Grafe audited their facilities last year.  After that audit, all SAP studies got preferential treatment, and judging from Stephen Yobar, some pretty good studies got short shrift in favor of SAP.

Stephen Yobar?

Yeah.  He worked with the vic.

That's some kind of coincidence.

You think?

Was SAP paying the vic off?

Not that we can find, but we'll keep looking.  Could be cash payoffs but it's possible he was getting opiate pills and selling them as you so expertly documented.  Their clinical trials tracked the social network of vets with opiate addictions and with PTSD.  Some of those vets are known to hang out at the *Flat Fifth* where you took those pictures.

Silence.

So that makes me think that maybe one of the vets he was selling to, or one of their family, was getting some revenge by killing Grafe.

Silence.

Who is your client?

My client didn't do it.  A spear, for God's sake.  And a fratlatl or something.

Who is your client?

I don't think that they were involved.

That's for me to decide.

Silence.

We're interviewing the wait staff at the *Flat Fifth*, what a stupid name, to see if we can identify any of Grafe's customers.  Maybe some of them used a credit card for dinner.

It used to be called the *Sharp Fourth*, you know.

Silence.

I thought I'd give that one another chance.  Can't blame me for trying, I'm a Renaissance detective.

Silence.

Detective Roberts, since you don't seem to be buying coincidences, what's the connection between those two Yobars and this case?

Shrugs.  Yobar the Elder works part-time at Grafe's company and told me about the SAP setup with the drugs.  Then, coincidentally, the murder weapon winds up in Yobar the Younger's car.  What's your client's name?

Silence.

You're going to be a jailed Renaissance detective if I need your client's name and you don't cough it up exactly when I need it. And those better be all the damn pictures.

He stood. Thanks for giving me some time. I've got to get back to my bike. I forgot to close the app so the meter is running.

Detective Roberts got up and closed his door after the private detective left. He sat down and swiveled his chair to look out the window. What is all this with the Yobars? Why kill somebody with a spear thrown by a whatsis?

The best lead seemed to be the angle on the opiates. He ran it down for himself: Grafe goes on a site audit for a clinical trial on PTSD and opiate use. He comes across a list of self-reported meeting places for vets with PTSD and opiate problems. Somehow, Grafe cuts a deal with the pharma company to fast-track their trials at the IRB and in return Grafe gets opiates that were reported to the FDA as destroyed. Harder to trace than money.

Grafe's burner phone still had a GPS tracker so the search warrant will show the pattern of sales that Grafe was making over the past few months. The *Flat Fifth* was on the list of meeting places so that fit. Yobar the Elder makes contact with SAP and a couple days later the murder weapon shows up in Yobar the Younger's car.

The connection is with Danny and Stephen. Clearly, one of them has an enemy. A lethal enemy.

# Chapter 18

It was 4PM so Ivan walked into his office to officially start the evening shift, even though he had been at Parizade's for several hours.  He closed his door to stand in front of his full mirror.  His black shoes were shined.  Tuxedo pants creased to perfection.  Dark shirt, dark tie, dark blue jacket.  His face angled up from his chin to his European haircut, close on the sides with a slight pompadour.  Gray hair accented his bright grey-eyed smile.

He glided from his office, past the bar, through the kitchen, greeting staff, to the stand at the front door.  A reservation list was loaded for the evening, and the sealed plastic map of the tables was already beginning to be filled in.

At eight, Stephen, Merrimac, and Danny walked through the doors and up to the maître'd stand.

Ivan greeted them with hands clasped forward and a warm welcoming.

"Welcome to Parizade's, my friends.  Do you have a reservation?"

Stephen said, "No, we thought we would see if there were a table available in the courtyard.  Is there any music in the courtyard tonight?  Ivan, you remember my son and Merrimac?"

"Of course!  You look beautiful tonight, Merrimac," he leaned in for an air kiss.  "That is a beautiful blouse you are wearing."  He shook hands with Danny.  "No reservations?  You are lucky, yes there is a table available in the courtyard," Ivan said with a smile.  "I believe Danny has played there before.  Please follow me."

The courtyard had a few trees and bushes lining the paving stones.  The trees were draped in white Christmas tree lights.  Involuntarily, Stephen gave a shiver because those lights reminded him of Christmas tree stands.

As Ivan handed them their menus, Stephen asked, "Do you have your corn dish?  First corn is the best corn, followed by the next corn." Ivan bowed and then went back to his station.

Merrimac looked at the diners around them and they had all finished their meals. "That's a shame everyone's done eating," Merrimac told Stephen. "I like to see what the food looks like before I order." Stephen glanced around and noticed that other diners had empty dishes and they seem to have entered the smart phone course of the meal. One lucky person was still eating their bananas Napoleon.

Danny hadn't said anything yet so Stephen tried to draw him out.

"Tell us more about your interview with Detective Roberts." Stephen and Merrimac both focused on Danny intently.

Danny let out a sigh. "Like I said, he came to the school to talk to me. He told me that they had gotten a tip that a murder weapon was in my car. It's the murder of that guy that worked with you at the IRB, Dad. Detective Roberts asked if he could look inside and I said yes. He searched it and he found a spear and some rock or stone hidden in the trunk under the carpet and on top of the spare tire. I told him they weren't mine and I didn't know how they got there. He should believe me, I mean, he knows me from when I almost got run over."

Stephen was quiet. Merrimac said consolingly, "That's awful, Danny. I'm so sorry this is happening."

Stephen followed up, "What else did he ask you?"

Danny had a little bit of a scared look on his face. "Yeah, he did have some more questions. He asked me if I had ever taught the bow and arrow camp at the Durham Friends School summer sessions, and I said yes. He acted like he already knew that so he must have researched me. I told him that I also taught the comic book writing camp, and helped in the music camp. Then he said I reminded him of you." He stopped for a moment. "He told me that he believed me and not to worry too much. So I'm trying not to think about it."

After a moment of silence, Stephen asked, "How are things between you and Mrs. Caruso?"

Danny's face fell further, rather than being happy at the change of subject. "We're not doing too well now. Her ex is giving her a lot of grief about us; he's the jealous type she says. I haven't met him and I don't want to. He's always lurking around her house and she's sure he was the school parent who told Dr. Nygren about us. She wants us to keep our distance for a while. And before you ask, Dr. Nygren let me know in no uncertain terms that he wasn't happy about our relationship and he was evaluating whether or not he would renew my contract for next year."

They placed their order and then waited in silence until their waiter delivered their drinks. After a quick cheers clinking of their glasses, Stephen decided to really change the subject. "At the data managers user group meeting, they posted a data management opening at *Syneos* and it said that a statistics degree was acceptable. A statis*tician*, can you believe that?"

Merrimac indicated that yes, should actually could believe that. Stephen turned an astonished face to Danny and said, "Statisticians think spreadsheets are databases!

Why would you give a database job to a statistician? If you broke your hand, you wouldn't get a foot doctor to operate on it, would you? There's a reason why there are specialists – use the right one for the job."

Danny seemed to ponder this. "Maybe I'm not the right fit for the Spanish gig at Durham Friends School, anymore. I'm more interested in IT and art these days than in Spanish. Like Dad says, you shouldn't give a hand job to a foot guy, right?"

Stephen spit out his beer and started choking and Danny started turning red.

"And what exactly are you laughing at?" Merrimac asked Stephen sternly.

"I was thinking about this joke I heard recently," Stephen rallied. "It's an old joke, but I still think it's funny." Danny kept a close eye on his dad to see how he got out of this.

Stephen started the joke, "Did you hear that the Invisible Man turned down the job offer?"

Blank stare from Merrimac.

"He couldn't see himself doing it."  Stephen raised his eyebrows, rather hopefully.

"OK, that's pretty good," Merrimac conceded.  She looked over at Danny for confirmation.

Danny wasn't paying much attention now.  He was having trouble on three fronts: the principal was upset with him about his relationship with Mrs. Caruso, Mrs. Caruso didn't want to see him now because of her ex, and the police think he is involved with a murder.

*Danny was in the pilot couch of his spaceship which was approaching Jupiter.  As captain, he was mulling his two options of how to use Jupiter's gravity: he can either sling himself back to Earth or hurl him towards even faster towards Saturn.  Either way, slingshotting around Jupiter will transfer energy from Jupiter to Danny's spaceship. Jupiter, as a result, will rotate just a bit more slowly but that's the way life goes.*

*On the radar, he saw an unknown ship following his trajectory, shadowing him.  Friend or foe?  He couldn't tell.*

*Saturn – it's so far away!  But the problem isn't that space is so big, it's that the speed of light is the maximum speed allowed and it's so slow[20].  Who cares if Saturn is a billion miles away if you can get there in 10 days by going much, much faster than the speed of light?  He fell back on the old stand-by: I don't make the rules, I just follow them.*

*He nodded his head to himself and put his inherited half-smirk on his face, a gesture of acceptance, a decision made.  He spoke to the computer which calculated and laid in the orbit.  It was a little more dangerous circling Jupiter for longer than the return trip home, but hey, that's what it takes to head to Saturn.*

"I think I'm going to move to Charlotte," Danny told them.

---

[20] Even in space, Dad is haunting me.

# Chapter 19

So my dealer shows up dead in the woods. That doesn't bother me. People kill people, people die. That's actually the one thing that's the same in Afghanistan and back home. I either have to find another dealer or go into rehab. It won't be hard to get a new connection.

My sister really wants me to go to rehab, but I don't know if I can. Life here is pretty dull and pointless as it is. The best thing I've got going is gardening. If I have to stop using, it's only going to be worse. She's coming over tonight for dinner with me and the parents. She'll just keep looking at me all night, just like she knows how to do. Then she'll make Mom cry and Dad will just walk out of the room.

Where's that card? I kept it for a reason, I guess.

# Chapter 1A

It was the second Tuesday of the month and that meant it was IRB day for Stephen. The newly assigned chair for the board was Olivia Harrison, an anesthesiologist. For this meeting, Stephen was the primary reviewer for Dr. Keyen's clinical trial that had been previously tabled by PJ Grafe. Stephen arrived to the meeting early, as usual, got his boxed lunch, and sat at his regular corner seat. Unlike last month's meeting, there was no joking or banter.

Dr. Harrison ran the board through the agenda quickly and efficiently. Stephen's review was the last one of the meeting. He read from his notes carefully and presented his review of Dr. Keyen's study, pointing out what had been changed since the meeting last month. Many of the issues raised by Grafe last month were addressed in this revised submission. Dr. Keyen had convinced the Ptolemy brass that the issues that couldn't be fixed could be monitored more intensely to ensure that the clinical trial subjects' rights were being protected. Stephen proposed that data and safety monitoring board meetings should be held every three months, rather than six months, so that trends in adverse events could be identified more quickly. The secondary reviewer did not have any additional comments. Stephen asked the board if it had any questions for Dr. Keyen who was waiting outside. The board didn't.

Stephen made his motion. "I move to approve the clinical trial contingent on the implementation of the stipulations in the protocol and informed consent forms. DSMB meetings must be held every three months. The DSMB charter must meet minimum Ptolemy IRB standards. I recommend that we review the study again in seven months so that we can see the results of the first two DSMB meetings."

Dr. Julia Thiesen, a pharmacologist from Duke added to the board to replace Grafe's expertise, said, "Second."

Chairperson Harrison said, "We have a second. All in favor of the motion, say aye." All members of the board, including the two on the phone, said aye.

"Anyone wishing to abstain or vote no?" The room was silent.

"The motion passes," Olivia said. "Thanks everyone for all your work today. This meeting is adjourned. Can someone let Sutton in?"

Dr. Keyen came in as the board members were shutting down their computers and heading to the snack and drink table in the corner. Dr. Harrison informed him of the board's decision and then walked over to Stephen and got a drink. She asked Stephen, "Hey, isn't that word whatsis contest coming up soon? It's usually around this time of year if I recall."

Stephen responded a little sheepishly, "It's this Friday at *Motorco*. I don't know why I keep going, but it seems to amuse my son."

"Maybe with the beard gone, you'll have a better chance of winning!" Dr. Keyen ribbed Stephen, still ecstatic from his trial being approved.

Stephen stroked his missing beard. "At least I'll have two fans there. My son Danny and my girlfriend Merrimac."

Stephen and Dr. Keyen sat down at the table, ate M&M's, and drank their soft drinks. Stephen turned to Dr. Keyen and said, "Congratulations on the new clinical trial."

Dr. Keyen replied, "Thanks. I'm glad we found a way to get it approved. And thanks for your work on the review. I knew it would get approved this time - I have my good luck charm," he said pulling on a necklace with a few carved talismans on it.

"Anyway, congratulations on the trial," Stephen got up and started to pack his briefcase. He usually found Keyen's English accent pleasant to listen to, but it was somehow different today. With a few *Good luck on Friday!*s chasing him, Stephen left the meeting to head to the *Savvy Café* to meet Merrimac for coffee.

## Chapter 1B

Dear Ann,

I have to move away.  It's in Eric's best interest and mine.  I've got to get away from my ex-husband.  After he complained about Danny teaching Eric, the school came down hard on Danny and told him that it's not ethical for a school teacher to have a relationship with a school parent.  He said the principal told him that it could give the appearance that Eric might be treated too leniently, or was being held to a different standard than other students, neither of which was fair to Eric.  And now after this whole mess, it actually *could* affect Eric.  Plus it's clear my ex is getting crazier, it's time to go.

I will miss you, Ann.  You always gave me such great advice.  You were always concerned about *my* benefit first, something that I can't afford to do. You never encouraged me to act in haste when I was upset.  You never gave in and easily agreed with me when what I needed was a strong friend to disagree.  It's rare to have a friend as true as you.

I will miss Danny.  It's probably for the best.  He might still have lingering feelings for his ex-girlfriend, he might not be able to handle being around Eric more if we stayed together.  Who am I to complain?  My ex-husband is actively ruining things, no *might*s about it.  I'm starting to love him so that's even more scary.  And Eric will only get more attached to Danny each day.

I have to move away.  I'm selling the store and the house.  I will call you when I can. Hugs and love.

R

# Chapter 1C

How in the world did I end up here?

Stephen sat on the stage at *Motorco* a few minutes before the annual Durham Wordplay contest. He participated every year and every year it seemed like it was a good idea, but it turned out not to be. Danny's friend Caroline Dunord from the *Basset Bakery* was also up there, and he recognized other contestants from previous years.

*Motorco* was packed. The stage was at the end of the hall and it had chairs for the sixteen contestants. There was a podium with two microphone stands at center stage. Spectators filled every seat, every spot on the floor, and there was standing room only at the back. The bright lights actually helped him; he couldn't see the crowd but he did hear Danny and Merrimac's yells of support above the crowd when he was introduced.

The Wordmaster was a former Cambridge professor and jokingly claimed he hailed from Durham, England. He wore a purple robe and some type of purple hat that no doubt he would identify as a bonnet. He was reciting the rules to the audience, reading from his notes. It only reinforced Stephen's fear of being on stage when he could hear the Wordmaster's voice directly and also through the PA system. Much too close to the action.

"Each contestant will have up to 5 seconds to say a wordplay. Most wordplays are puns (single or multi-lingual), anagrams, palindromes. I am the judge as to whether a contestant's offering is sufficient or if it is disqualified because it either wasn't sufficiently *wordy* enough or it was too close to a wordplay already used this evening. If needed, I will ask the contestant for a clarification. If the wordplay is disqualified, the contestant will have another 3 seconds to come up with a new try. The first contestant to not provide a valid wordplay loses the round. All contestant pairings are selected at random. There are four rounds tonight, and in the event of a tie, each round will have a different tie-breaking method."

He stroked his white beard and then shuffled his cards. "The first two contestants are," looking through his glasses at his notes, "Stephen Yobar and Lettie Finnhaden."

Great, Stephen thought, as he heard chants of "Let-*tie*, Let-*tie*" in the crowd, she's got a cheering section.

Stephen and Lettie stood up and walked up to the microphone stands, Stephen on the left, Lettie on the right. When they were situated, the Wordmaster said, "The category is……. Automobiles. Get wordy!" he said as he pointed at Stephen.

Stephen looked into the lights and said into the mic, "My favorite car is *a Toyota*". The Wordmaster looked at him skeptically and Stephen said, "A Toyota. That's a palindrome." Stephen quickly tried to formulate his next try.

The Wordmaster nodded and turned to his opponent. She shot back, "My *nova* won't go anymore." The Wordmaster said, "Yes, a Spanish pun – no va – won't go! Very good." The laughs from the audience and the Wordmaster's stare told Stephen that it was his turn again.

"My girlfriend *raves* about her *Versa*." The time the Wordmaster said "Nice anagram, raves and Versa." Only 8 more to go, panicked Stephen, what the hell am I doing up here. Lettie had to explain her next pun which gave Stephen a few extra seconds. He had one ready.

At the right time, Stephen leaned into the mic to his mouth and said, "I had to steal a slate gray Tesla because my old car was too stale – but at least I don't tell tall tales." The Wordmaster said, "Bravo! Six anagrams on Tesla, not too shabby!" Stephen, hoping for extra credit, leaned into the mic and said, "Can you inscribe that on a stela for me?" The audience laughed.

Lettie apparently had no more wordplays or folded under the pressure, both of which happened to Stephen last year in round 2. This was much more difficult than just spouting out puns at random like he normally did.

Stephen sat down and was happy he had at least made it through the first round. He had practiced with Merrimac but it was different up here.

After the end of the first round, there was a break so that *Motorco* could sell some drinks. Stephen wandered down to the floor and Merrimac and Danny approached him.

"You're doing great!" Merrimac exclaimed and gave Stephen a kiss on the cheek.

"Well, it's been fun, but it's time to go," Stephen made a false step to the exit.

Danny grabbed his arm. "Come on Dad, you're doing great. You didn't even flinch when she stole that *no va* pun you've been saying for years. Besides, you've made it to the Elite Eight, not bad for an old man."

After the Wordmaster had settled the audience, he announced, "Let's get wordy!" Stephen was soon enough standing in front of the mic looking into the lights. His opponent this round was a newbie. The most dangerous kind of opponent.

"This round is a free-for-all," the Wordmaster explained, "your wordplay isn't restricted to a subject area, and there will be only 4 wordplays. All other rules apply." The Wordmaster flipped a coin, then pointed at Sarah and said, "Get wordy!"

Sarah: Chickens only like the fruit of the orange. The outside has no ap*peal* to them.

Stephen: *Her suit* had cat hair all over it. To the Wordmaster's questioning glance, Stephen answered, "Had hair. Like hirsute." The Wordmaster smiled and pointed to Sarah.

Sarah: Security at the LA airport was lax.

Stephen: I took my son shopping for a suit, socks, and shoes for his job interview – I said I'd pay for those. He also wanted one of those decorative handkerchiefs. I said if you want that, it's coming out of your pocket."

Sarah: 'I have a question about Chronos.' 'Well, it's about time!'

Stephen: My brother got a prosthesis from a non-profit company. It still cost him an arm and a leg.

Sarah: I need to *select* a SQL programmer. The Wordmaster grinned and nodded his head, saying, "I love the computer geeks!"

Stephen: He's got great arc on his jump shot. Then he got thrown out of the league for being on parabolic steroids.

The Wordmaster threw up his arm and declared, "It's a tie! For this round, the tie-breaker is a lightning round where the wordplay between the contestants is in response to each other. The limit is 3 seconds in this lightning round. The topic is...... Alaska!" He flipped his coin and pointed to Stephen, "Get wordy!"

Stephen: You better count your money on withdrawals because they don't have fair banks up there.

Sarah: Don't anchorage him with these bad puns.

Stephen: Juneau what the capital of Alaska is?

Sarah tried to come up with another, but the buzzer went off.

Stephen sat back in his chair and tried not to listen to the rest of the second round matchups.  The crowd seemed to like it though because they were really laughing.

Finally there were just four contestants sitting in the folding chairs on the stage.

The Wordmaster addressed the crowd.  "For our third, and dare I say *pun*ultimate, round between Stephen and Tom, the category is……International Money!"  He pointed at Tom, and said, "Get wordy!"

Tom: "I couldn't *weight* to buy *pesos* in Mexico."

Stephen: "I *baht* some souvenirs when I was in Bangkok."

Tom: "I got *pound*ed on the exchange rate in the UK."

Stephen: "I keep it *real* when I'm in Rio."  The Wordmaster explained to the crowd, which was quiet, "Real is the money in Brazil."

Tom: "*Frank*ly, I can't afford to visit Paris."

Stephen, looking for the knockout, pointing to Tom: "Is that *dong* in your pocket, or are you just happy to see me?"  The crowd laughed and then laughed again when the Wordmaster explained, "*Dong* is the money in Viet Nam.  Very good!"

Tom couldn't recover from change in momentum and didn't get out another attempt.

"Well done, contestants!  Stephen you move to the final round!"

Caroline was in the other semi-final and he wished her luck as they crossed paths on the stage.  Her semi-final went the full five wordplays, a tie, and she won by the having the crowd cheer louder for her than her opponent.

The final was set – Stephen versus Caroline.  One last chance to humiliate myself, Stephen thought.

The Wordmaster introduced the final two contestants to loud ovations from the crowd.

"The topic of our final round tonight, for the honor of being the *Wordster of the Year* is foreign language and foreign countries.  Now Stephen, that seems to be your category but Caroline has had a few tonight too.  Choosing at random", he flipped a coin and then pointed, "Caroline, get wordy!"

Caroline: "Once, when I was 11, I went on a Spanish immersion trip." To the Wordmaster's raised eyebrows, Caroline elaborated, "Once is *eleven* in Spanish."

Stephen: Is that Himalayan salt? - I wouldn't want Tibet on it.

The crowd laughed, including the Wordmaster.  "Good one Stephen!

"Caroline, go!" The Wordmaster was keeping the pace going.

"*Who's* been *keyin'* my car door?"

The Wordmaster gave her a look.  She said, "*Quien* is *who* in Spanish, so *who is keying my car*."  Satisfied, the Wordmaster turned to Stephen and said, "Go!"

"Who's keyin'" resonated in Stephen's head. In a flash, Stephen realized that Mrs. Caruso's ex-husband is – Dr. Keyen!

The logic unfolded quickly in Stephen's mind. The bloody spear, atlatl, and stone were put in Danny's car by the killer to frame Danny. The only person who would want to frame Danny was an enemy. The only enemy Danny had was Mrs. Caruso's ex-husband. Therefore, the ex-husband *was* the killer. Oh my God, that picture of the stone that Merrimac had was very similar to the stone talismans on Keyen's necklace at the IRB meeting. He wanted to make sure, remember that picture at the *Flip and Sip*? The picture from behind with the guy in costume shooting the arrow? Was it Keyen? He had to see it to confirm, and then tell Detective Roberts.

"Sorry, Stephen!" The Wordmaster announced at the buzzer. "You lose on time! But it looked like you were cooking up a whopper! Congratulations to the new Wordster of the Year - Caroline Dunord! Thank you to all the contestants tonight and to the *Motorco* staff! Good night, everyone! Caroline Dunord – Wordster of the

Year!" He lifted Caroline's right hand up in victory and she was smiling widely as the crowd cheered wildly. Stephen quickly shook her hand and got off-stage to see Merrimac and Danny.

"What happened up there, Dad? Foreign language puns are your specialty! You don't look too crushed though," Danny finished.

"I think I figured out who killed Grafe and who tried to frame you Danny! But first we need to get down to the *Flip and Sip* and confirm something I saw in one of the pictures there." They rushed out through the crowd and into the street.

# Chapter 1D

He walked into the *Flip and Sip* with his gym bag and scanned his membership card.   Silently he walked by the stalls where people were paying $20/hour to throw axes at a bullseye painted on wooden two by fours at the end of the stall.

Keyen walked to the back, past the bar, to the locker room, and opened his locker.  He changed into the buckskin clothes and carried his atlatl and spears that he had taken out of the locker.  He snuck out the back of the axe throwing establishment and took the back alleys until he was within sight of *Motorco*'s main entrance.  The venue was packed to overflowing and he could hear the laughter and applause.  He waited patiently across the street behind a food truck until the contest ended.

As the crowd started to leave, he placed the spear in the atlatl and held it in a crouch, one knee on the ground.

Stephen, Danny, and Merrimac came out of *Motorco*. They stopped on the corner while Stephen explained more why he thought he knew who the killer was and why they had to get down to the *Flip and Sip* to look at that picture one more time.

Next to *Motorco*, a group of twenty somethings were flying their drones in one of the few remaining empty lots. The drones were pretty quiet and you couldn't hear them unless they were pretty low.  Four drones were racing around the telephone and utility poles on the street.  They took the corners around the track pretty close and one almost hit the pole in front of *Motorco*.  Danny lifted his arm and pointed to an out of control drone coming right at them.

Keyen lifted the spear-loaded atlatl and launched the spear towards Danny.  It smashed into the drone!

Detective Roberts was waiting behind a row of Leyland cypresses across the street from *Motorco*.  After the murder weapon was planted in Danny's car, he thought Danny was his best lead so he had followed him all day.  As Danny, Stephen, and Stephen's girlfriend came out of

*Motorco,* he looked left down Rigsbee St. and saw Keyen crouching behind a food truck. After his shock at seeing a man in buckskin clothes actually using an atlatl to launch a spear across the street and hit the drone, Detective Roberts came out from the cypresses and shouted.

"Drop that atlatl!"

The detective issued his command while holding out his badge. He pointed his service revolver at the man dressed in animal skins holding an atlatl in one hand and a spear in the other.

The buckskinned man shouted back with a British accent.

"Atl be the day!"

He put the spear in the atlatl and was bringing the atlatl forward with a murderous velocity towards Danny when the detective shot him in his right arm. The atlatl and Keyen dropped harmlessly to the ground.

# Chapter 1E

Stephen got to the police station at 2PM and by 4PM he was ready to sign his statement. Detective Roberts and Stephen sat in the conference room while Stephen read his typed statement. Roberts didn't like the quiet so talked while Stephen read.

"We knew that Grafe was selling the drugs and I thought that that was the best motive for his murder, but when the murder weapons turned up in your son's car, that threw me for a loop. Your son has no direct link to Grafe so it must be you the murderer was trying to put off. Following Danny was my best bet then, I thought."

Roberts admonished Stephen, "It would have been better if Danny had mentioned his problems with his girlfriend. Especially when it turns out that his girlfriend's ex was the one who narced to his principal, planted the murder weapons in his car, and tried to kill him with a freaking atlatl." Stephen quietly continued reading his statement.

Roberts toned down the heated glance he had on Stephen, seeing as how Stephen had helped with the case. "It turns out that Dr. Keyen's and Mrs. Caruso's son had a rare blood disease. With proper treatment, the son was leading a normal life – Danny said he didn't even know about it. My guess is that Keyen thought that he could win back his ex if he could get some successes with the pediatric blood disease clinical trial. That doesn't make much sense, but when he checked into the hospital, he admitted that he has been off his bipolar meds for the past six months or so."

Stephen said, while still reading his statement, not sure if it was safe yet to raise his eyes, "So that's why he was so upset about his clinical trials getting turned down by PJ?"

Roberts shrugged and said, "We'll see what he has to say, if he says anything at all. My guess again is that Keyen probably felt guilty thinking that his bipolar issues had something to do with his son's hereditary disease. That doesn't make much sense either, but I think Keyen was coming off the rails pretty good. The forensic team says that Keyen could be very unpredictable off his meds."

Stephen looked up at that. "Unpredictable? You think? Like wearing buckskins and throwing spears at his enemies with a freaking atlatl?"

Detective Roberts pointed a finger at Stephen and replied, "Don't get an attitude with me. My guess is that once Keyen got Grafe out of the way, and his pediatric cancer trial was approved, he was probably feeling pretty invincible. Unfortunately, he perceived your son was in his way to reuniting with his ex. That's the only thing I can think of that makes sense. Getting Danny fired from the Durham Friends School wasn't enough, he wanted to frame him for the murder, which of course is ridiculous. And that still wasn't enough – he wanted to kill Danny. Until the murderer planted the weapon's in your son's car, my money was on Timothy Simon from SAP. Or even one of the vets or the vet's family members. We've tied three overdoses of vets to the opiate signature in the SAP drugs. Simon will be going away for a while on federal drug charges. Also, the DA is also looking to set some precedent by charging him with second degree murder for the deaths of the vets."

Stephen flipped through the statement one last time as Roberts continued. "There are also the charges for falsifying FDA drug disposal documentation." Roberts smiled big now. "Of course, since you participated in that particular fraud in conjunction with our investigation, you won't be charged Stephen. Just checking, but you did turn in all the opiates that Simon gave you?"

Stephen looked up after signing his statement and saw the rare smile on the detective's face. "I can't believe I was the one who told Keyen that Danny would be at the contest that night," Stephen lamented.

Roberts leaned back as far as the chair would go and stretched his arms. "We found a bunch of those atlatls and spear points at Keyen's house and in his locker at the axe place," the detective concluded. "He had quite a collection of flint points. I hate to say, but he got what he deserved and he got off lucky."

"You didn't have a choice," Stephen said looking him in the eye. "And if I didn't say thank you for saving Danny's life, I'm saying it now."

Roberts pointed at his right shoulder. "I got him right in the atlatl throwing arm."

Roberts confirmed that the statement was signed and dated, and started walking Stephen to the exit.

"What else is going on with you these days?[21] I notice you're still seeing that same woman? Isn't she a bit young for you?" Roberts smirked.

"Yes," Stephen replied, "but she's catching up with me."

---

[21] 
| | |
|---|---|
| Week 2 of 8 | hair cut |
| Day 17 of 40 | shaving cream supply |
| Day 3 of 3 | having to shave |
| Day 22 of 37 | toothpaste |
| Day 22 of 185 | tooth brush life |
| Year 32 of 40 | working |
| Year 2 of 10 | life of car |
| Mile 2550 of 3000 | oil change |
| Mile 175 of 375 | miles left in tank |
| Year 1 of 2.5 | shoes |
| Month 1 of 4 | clean refrigerator |
| Day 2 of 5 | going to work this week |
| 45 minutes | time left in 3 hour parking zone |

# Chapter 1F

Danny was just returning to Stephen's couch after making the refrigerator one beer lighter. He heard the knock on the door and guessed that it was Merri. He looked to the back of the house to see if his father had heard the door and was going to answer it. Seeing that he wasn't, Danny opened the door and let in both Merri and a cool rain. She dropped her bags and started to shake off the rain.

"'How wild the wind blows on this summer's eve'," Danny poemed to Merri, channeling his father's deep voice into the made-up poem as he closed the door against the summer solstice night.

Danny realized just how wild the weather was when he looked at Merri. Her hair was bunched up around the scarf that double wrapped her neck, hairs protruding awkwardly up to give her mouth cover. She scrunched her reddened face. She put down some to-go bags and quickly took off her drenched raincoat. When she took off her knit cap, Danny almost laughed when static electricity made her hair stand on end like a cartoon character.

"You'll warm up soon, Merri. The fire is really going. Dad loves to have roaring fires at his Solstice Parties, even if it is the summer solstice."

Stephen came into the room in and approached Merrimac. Fine strands of her hair were dancing around her head like an aurora. The scarf she had gotten on a monitoring trip to Brazil framed her face beautifully. Her long hair was pushed up and out from her jacket, brunette highlights glowing warm from the overhead light. Her dark eyebrows and red cheeks doomed his next attempt at a breath. He hoped it would come back as he approached her and she smiled at him.

"Isn't it a beautiful evening?" he asked as he hugged her.

She released the hug and picked up the to-go bags in her right hand. "I brought some shrimp and dip for an appetizer and some desserts from *The Daily Churn*.

Caroline said it's a consolation prize for coming in second at the wordplay contest."

Stephen smiled and Danny added, "Dad can't have shrimp because of his situation."

"What situation?" Merrimac was beginning to get the hang of these conversations. She looked at Danny.

"His crustacean situation."

Merrimac laughed and turned to Stephen, "I assume that he means an allergy to shrimp?" She put her hand on his shoulder.

Stephen nodded. "Come on in. I was just to put on *Kind of Blue*, a total classic."

Danny thought he'd beat his father to the punch. "Merri, it's the notes that Miles *doesn't* play that makes him so great." He smiled at his dad.

Not to be outdone, Stephen added, "Not just that, Danny; it's the *way* he doesn't play those notes that makes him a genius."

"So what have you been up to today?" Merrimac asked Stephen in the polite tone that people use when they are hanging up their jacket and are stalling for time. She then put the bags of food on the kitchen counter. She went to the refrigerator and opened a bottle of chardonnay.

"Mostly XML programming today. I feel like I'm seeing tags everywhere I look. And letters are starting to look like ASCII codes."

Stephen put the shrimp and dip on a large platter and walked it down to the green felt tablecloth-covered table in the living room. He arranged the platter and another side plate of snacks. He eased himself into the corner of the couch, sipping his beer, hoping that Merrimac would take the seat next to him. Which she did.

Merrimac took a sip of wine and looked at the trophies on the mantle over the fireplace.

"Tell me about those trophies, Stephen. Data manager of the year awards?" She nudged him with a smile.

"Hah. Danny was a great soccer player in junior high," Stephen said. "He had great scamperability. Also, his right foot was considered a legend at the time."

Danny, happy to hear his dad brag about him and eager to not show it too much, said to Merrimac, "My dad has no limits. He loves to say that my foot was a legend[22] because a foot actually is a *leg end*. This is what I deal with every time I see him, as you well know."

Merrimac laughed a loud laugh. "That's not the worst thing a father could do!"

Danny pressed his point, "Merrimac, believe it or not, my dad still believes that Elvis is alive!"

Stephen looked at Merrimac and defended himself, "Well, anagrammically at least, *Elvis lives*!"

Danny finished his beer and fought the good fight. "'Anagrammically' isn't a word, Dad!"

"*That*," Stephen extended his right arm and pointed his finger at Danny, "is what you said about *uncontinental*,

---

[22] See Appendix

and you were wrong about *that*, my young man," he ended with another jab.

"I wasn't wrong about that!" Danny turned to Merrimac for support. "*Uncontinental* isn't a word, but that's not the worst part, Merri. Do you *really* want to know the worst part?"

Merrimac looked at Danny and did not respond.

"And I mean the *worst* part!" Danny dared her to answer.

She declined.

Stephen did a slow burn and said very officially to Danny, "Your manners are very uncontinental, my son."

"Dad, don't try to use it. It's not a word."

Danny turned his gaze back to Merrimac. "You better tell her why you want it to be a word, Dad. She wouldn't believe me."

"First of all, it is a word.  It means the opposite of continental, as in, *I wish my son didn't have such uncontinental manners*," Stephen asserted again.

"It's not a word."

"Yes, it is."

Merri laughed and interrupted. "OK – why does it even matter if it's a word or not?"  She looked at both of them.

Danny got a very satisfied look on his face and leaned back in his chair.  With a wave of his hand, "That's right, Dad.  Explain *why* it matters that it's a word."

Stephen was quiet, still a rare phenomenon to Merrimac.

"Well?" she pressed.

Stephen cleared his throat.  "You see, it's like this.  If uncontinental were a word," Stephen turned and looked directly at Danny, "and it *is* my boy, it *is*, well if it were a word then..."

"Oh, for God's sake," Danny interrupted.

Stephen soldiered on. "It's the only word I can think of that has the all the vowels going backwards in it, u o i e a. Uncontinental."

After a few beats of silence, Merrimac stood up and announced, "I'll get the desserts!"

Merrimac was determined to change the subject as she returned from the kitchen carrying a platter with small bowls of dessert and so she offered, "'The Daily Churn' had two specials today. Mexican chocolate ice cream and an orange sherbet. I also brought their chocolate pound cake. Which would you like, Danny?"

Before Danny could answer, Stephen volunteered still stuck in XML-land, "<pun>It's a <homonym>sure bet</homonym> Danny will choose ice cream</pun>."

<laughs and groans> Merrimac distributed a bowl of Mexican ice cream to Danny</laughs and groans>.

Stephen said, "And I'll have the chocolate <pun><homonym> # </homonym></pun>cake, thank you Merrimac."

In between bites of pound cake, Stephen asked Danny, "Do you have any job interviews lined up?"

Danny responded, "I just had an in-person interview for a Spanish position at the Charlotte Latin Institute of Technology."

Choosing just the right tone of voice, a mix of wanting things to go well for his son but not sounding like he wanted his son to move to Charlotte, Stephen took another bite of cake and asked, "Well, how do you think it went? Did you get a good vibe?"

Danny frowned. "Pretty soon into the interview, I kept changing the topic from the Spanish gig to the fact that I could also help run their network, keep their website up to date, teach drums in their jazz band. Dr. Nygren would give me a good recommendation for *that* at least, I'm sure. But I think I rubbed them the wrong way. So I don't think it's going to happen."

Danny finished his ice cream and stood up. Three was definitely becoming a crowd. "On that note....." Danny took his dishes to the kitchen. Stephen and Merrimac walked him to the door and everyone hugged and said good night.

Stephen put a few more pieces of wood on the fire and sat back down on the couch, extending his knee before it had the chance to freeze up.

Merrimac: Would you pine for me in my absence?

Stephen:                                                    Yes.

After a few moments, Stephen ASCII'd, "73 32 76 111 118 101 32 121 111 117."

"I can't believe you said that," she responded quietly.

Merrimac moved closer to Stephen than before, held Stephen's hand and said, "I'm so happy here. I'm glad I'm not thinking of having to move away to Charlotte or somewhere."

Stephen told her, "You are such a beautiful person. So many people would miss you. But that would be true wherever you go, whatever you do. Charlotte or wherever."

"Now you're making me cry."

Stephen smiled gently at her. "Emotion's good. I wish I could cry more."

He kissed her cheek, nuzzling up to her ear.

Eyes closed, with a whisper, "My Merrimac."

Sighing sweet susurrations, soft she swooned.

# Appendix

Step/hen collects words that meet the following criteria:

- Compound words in which the words that make up the compound word have nothing to do with the compound word.

    o   E.g., car/pet

- Each of the compound words must have at least two letters.

- Personal names or names of places don't count.

- Words from other languages that are normal English words do count, like 'mandate'.

- Words that need apostrophes but don't have them in the compound word are acceptable. Contractions count, like hes, without the apostrophe

- Onomatopoeia words are legitimate English (ting, ding)

Ad/age
Ad/or/able
All/owed
All/owing

Am/bit/ion
Amen/able
Ant/hem, an/them
An/tic
An/us
Are/as
Am/end
An/gel
An/tit
An/tit/hes/is
An/tip/as/to
App/ear
Arc/tic
Arm/or
Arm/our
As/certain
Ash/ore
Asp/halt
Asp/ire
As/say
As/sass/in/ate
As/sent
As/set
As/sign
As/sure
At/one
At/tack
At/tempt
At/tend
At/ten/dance
At/test
At/tic
Bad/i/age

Band/age
Ban/died
Bar/gain
Ban/king
Bar/king
Bar/on
Bar/row
Bat/her
Bat/on
Bat/ten
Be/an
Be/at
Be/gin
Be/have
Best/owed
Be/tray, bet/ray
Bin/go
Bog/us
Bran/dish
Brie/fly
Bud/get
But/ton
Cam/pus
Can/did
Can/did/ate
Car/dig/an
Can/teen
Car/go
Car/nation
Carp/ark
Carp/enter
Carp/entry, car/pen/try
Car/pet

Car/rot
Car/ton
Cart/ridge
Cast/rate
Cave/at
Comb/in/at/ion
Con/firm/at/ion
Con/flag/rat/ion
Coven/ant
Cove/rage
Crow/ding
Dam/age
Dam/nit
Deter/mine
Dig/it
Dis/aster
Dis/cover
Dis/grunt/led
Dish/evel/ed
Do/cent
Do/me
Domes/tic/ate
Don/ate
Don/or
Do/nut
Do/or
Do/sage
Do/use
Do/wager
Drag/on
Ear/nest
Emu/late
Era/sure

Fart/her
Far/ting
Fat/her
Feat/her
Fin/ally
Fin/ding
Flag/on
For/age
For/get
For/got
For/mat
For/tune
For/ward
Gab/led
Garb/age
Garb/led
Gar/den
Gat/her
Gene/rally
Gig/antic, gig/an/tic
Go/at
Go/of
Go/on
Go/red
Go/ring
Hall/owed
Hand/some
He/arse
He/at
He/at/hen
He/at/her
He/don/is/tic
Her/it/age

Her/on
Her/ring
Hes/it/ant
Hes/it/ate
Hi/red
Hi/story
Hit/her/to
Hone/sty
Host/age
Hum/an
In/crease
Imp/rove
Imp/roved
Import/ant
In/got
In/he/rent
In/for/m/at/ion, in/form/at/ion
In/no/vat/ion
In/tent
In/tense
In/tern/at/ion/ally
Is/sue
Is/suing
Jar/ring
Just/ice
Lab/or
Lad/led
Lap/sing
Late/rally
Leg/end
Leg/it/im/ate
Less/on
Lit/he

Lot/ion
Lot/us
Ma/lady
Man/date
Mar/bled
Mar/bling
Mar/gin
Marg/in/ally
Mar/in/ate
Mar/king
Mar/row
Mar/shall
Mar/shy
Mass/age
May/hem
Me/ant
Me/an
Me/at
Men/ace
Men/ding
Mess/age
Men/tally
Miss/ion
Mode/rate
Mum/my
Nog/gin
No/mad
No/on
No/table, not/able
Not/at/ion
Not/ice
Not/ion
No/vice

Now/here
Off/end
Off/ice
Of/ten
On/ion
On/us
Or/at/or
Or/bit
Pain/ting
Pal/ace
Pa/late
Pal/met/to
Pane/list
Pan/the/on
Pant/her
Pan/try
Par/able
Par/don
Par/king
Par/rot
Par/tying
Pass/ion
Pass/ion/ate
Pat/tern
Pat/riot
Pen/ding
Peas/ant
Pen/is
Per/son/ally
Pet/it/ion
Pick/led
Plan/tar
Pleas/ant

Plea/sing
Plea/sure
Pot/ion
Prim/ate
Quest/ion
Ram/page, ram/page
Ram/pant, ramp/ant
Ram/part, ramp/art
Ran/king
Rap/port
Rat/her
Rat/ion
Rat/ion/ale
Red/act
Rendition
Rest/art
Rest/ore
Rid/dance
Rot/ate
Rot/at/or
Rug/by
Sat/is/faction
Sea/led
Sea/red
Sea/ring
Sea/son
Sew/age
Shall/owed
She/riff
Sin/king
Slat/her
Slit/her
So/lace

So/lute
So/me
So/on
So/use
So/wing
Span/king
Spar/king
Star/ting
Sub/miss/ion
Sun/dry
Surge/on
Tab/led
Tab/let
Tab/led
Tail/or
Tan/king
Tar/get
Ten/don, tend/on
Tea/ring
Tea/sing
Than/king
The/me
The/sis
Thin/king
Thou/sand
Tick/led
To/get/her
To/me
Tom/or/row
To/tally, tot/ally
To/wing
Trait/or
Under/stand

Under/stood
Us/age
Us/her
Vine/gar
Wag/on
Wall/owed
War/den
War/rant
Was/her
We/at/her
We/stern
Whet/her
Win/ding
Win/king
Win/some
Wit/her
Wit/he/ring
Who/red
Who/ring

## Anagrams that have recently caught Stephen's eye

Notes/stone/tones

Stare/rates/tears/tares

Crate/cater/trace/react

Staple/plates/pleats/pastel

Spread/drapes/spared

Stop, spot, tops, opts, post, pots

## Palindromes that Stephen noticed on presentations at work

Part/trap

Regal/lager

No parts strap on

Spat/taps

tram/mart

Remit/timer

Edit/tide

Swap/paws

Smug/gums

Smart/trams

Snub/buns

Snug/guns

Pins/snip

Snap/pans   naps/span (anagramic palindromes)

Stab/bats   (plus tabs)


## Things that bother Stephen

The plural of Trader Joe stores should be Traders Joe, not Trader Joes


## Triple/Quadruple Homonyms

by, bye, buy
cite, sight, site
cent, sent, scent
I, eye, aye
sew, so, sow
chord, cored, cord
do, dew, due
need, knead, kneed
oar, or, ore, o'er (4)
peek, peak, pique
pore, poor, pour
you, yew, ewe
to, too, two
for, four, fore

so, sow, sew
seas, sees, seize
toed, toad, towed
where, ware, wear
load, lode, lowed
road, rode, rowed
way, weigh, whey

## Spelled the same, pronounced different

bow
conduct
conflict
construct
estimate
frequent
learned
moderate
polish
object
produce
project
record
resign
row
subject
suspect
wind

## Noun and a verb

water
plant
drink
draft
drum
crown
comment
cook
crowd
drill
group
hammer
ice
iron
judge
brush
pin
farm
form
mix
record
salt
sample
seal
ship
signal
sprinkle
sum
tape
trash

process
pull
file
question
plan
wish
wrinkle